GRAY
AREA

Other books by Linda M. Au

Novel:

The Scarlet Letter Opener

Humor Essays:

Head in the Sand . . . and other unpopular positions
Fork in the Road . . . and other pointless discussions

GRAY AREA

A NOVEL

LINDA M. AU

vicious
circle
publishing

Vicious Circle Publishing
PO Box 133
New Brighton, PA 15066-0133
viciouscirclepublishing.com
twitter.com/ViciousCirclePb
viciouscirclepublishing@gmail.com

For:

Fara Howell Pienkosky, for her unfiltered, honest opinions and love

Lynne Gordon, for being my first beta reader in years past

*Jim W. and Lora Z., for making sure I didn't boldly go
where no woman has gone before*

*Crit Club, for more collective help than I could afford
if I had to pay you guys*

*The RPCNA, the best support group a gal could ever hope to have
in times of trouble*

PART ONE: BLACK

Q. 81. *Are all true believers at all times assured of their present being in the estate of faith, and that they shall be saved?*

A. Assurance of faith and salvation not being of the essence of faith, true believers may wait long before they obtain it; and, after the enjoyment thereof, may have it weakened and intermitted, through manifold distempers, sins, temptations, and desertions; yet are they never left without such a presence and support of the Spirit of God, as keeps them from sinking into utter despair.

—*The Westminster Larger Catechism*, Question 81

1

Behold, I cry out, 'Violence!' but I am not answered;
I call for help, but there is no justice.

—Job 19:7

D IRT FILLS MY NOSE AND I GAG, my face pushed into the
ground and held there.
    "Lie still!"

My mind races for other options. I have none. I'm prostrate on the grimy ground, and he's sitting heavy on my back, one hand pressing my face into the dirt, the other holding my right arm twisted painfully behind my back. Adrenaline buzzes in my ears, and I wonder briefly if I'm going to faint from the wash of it in my veins. My stomach churns with a paralyzing panic that keeps me from screaming or defending myself. I won't get any words or sound past the huge, throbbing pulse in my throat.

Where is my purse? My phone. I desperately need the phone. I try to turn my head a little to find where I must have dropped it nearby, but his hand thrusts my face hard onto the ground again, where my nose finds a bit of rock and strikes it just right to make it bleed. I choke and try to snuff the blood outward and not sniffle it back up my nose.

"Don't you know what 'lie still' means? Quit it or else!"

I smell the warm blood seeping from my nose and begin to cry again. Wordless, soundless sobbing, the kind that won't get me into more trouble.

"Please, don't ..." I stick on my own words and the sobs become audible. Maybe all he wants is the purse. Maybe he already knows where it is. Maybe he threw it off into the bushes down the side of the hill so I can't get to it. Doesn't matter. No purse, no phone, no hope. *Oh, God, dear God, no hope.* The racking sobs grow louder, turning to animal wails of delirium.

"Now you've gone and done it. It's your fault I have to do this."

My mind scrambles to make sense of what he said, of how any of this could possibly be my fault, and my eyes roll upward and to the left instinctively, trying to see something other than the rocks and dry blades of grass nearest to my face. His hand leaves my head for a moment, and in my panicked confusion I cock my head suddenly left to see why I've been granted the reprieve. As I lift my head away from the ground and feel clumps of dirt fall away from my right cheek, I see him raise his free hand up over his head, an enraged, insane look on his face.

It is the last thing I see that day. Or the next.

+ + + + +

I KEPT MY EYES CLOSED, letting the sunshine warm my eyelids for a while. Lying quietly on an antiseptic bed, I listened, motionless and feigning sleep. Low, muffled voices drifted through a door or wall—maybe a half dozen people or less. The faint odor of pine and lemon, not an entirely unpleasant combination in small doses, wafted my way.

Louder than the hushed voices was a high-pitched beep, rhythmic and steady. No, a ping. *Ping. Ping. Ping.* It came from across the room, behind it a raspy breathing pattern. I wasn't alone.

By now I was too curious and opened my eyes to find a hospital room, with an old Hispanic woman attached to a monitor sleeping in the bed next to me. With my heart pounding wildly, I tried to sit up to get a better look around, but a walloping pain slammed my temples. The pain smacked me back down onto the bed. Gingerly touching my forehead, I found it swollen and tender. The entire left side of my face felt puffy. I bit my jaw down and a sharp little pain slung itself up from my jaw to my eye. *Don't do that again, stupid.*

I gave up assessing the room and continued to assess my body instead, finding various cuts and scrapes all along my right side: shoulder, torso, upper leg, a nasty bruised and smarting area around my right knee. I didn't ask myself how or why this happened. This was beginning to seem less and less like something I wanted to remember. The aching pain, though. It was seeping out all my pores. And I was too weary to process it right.

A few muffled voices were right at the door now, and I shouted, "Nurse!" My voice cracked. The Hispanic woman next to me stirred a little, rattling a cough that frightened me, and settled back into a breathing pattern that sounded like sleep.

The door opened and a young woman in a crisp, white uniform stepped in.

"Oh, you're awake!" she said, somewhat surprised. "Let me get the doctor." And, as suddenly as she appeared, she let the door close behind her and was gone.

I sighed and slumped back down flat on the bed. Not the kind of bed to curl up in to read a good book on a chilly fall afternoon. It was emotionally uncomfortable here. Suddenly I wanted to be anywhere but here.

The door swung open again and in stepped a middle-aged man with graying temples and the same nurse who made the cameo appearance a few moments earlier.

"Well, you're awake," he said.

"I'd feel better if you told me this is a dream." My voice quivered with telltale signs of distress. He might be used to hearing this sort of inflection, but I certainly wasn't.

"Wish I could do that, but no, it's real. But I'm glad to see you awake and alert. I'm Dr. Camp." He smiled a very soothing, rehearsed bedside-manner smile, apparently in no hurry to tell me what happened.

"What happened to me?" I asked, not up for a Muzak-induced conversation. I felt defensive and was too busy fighting the rising swell of panic again. "Please just tell me what happened."

He stopped smiling. "How much do you remember of what happened?"

"What do you mean, what do I remember?" I fought back tears and realized I was making little choking sounds in my effort to keep from sobbing outright. There was apparently a lot to remember.

"Please, I meant nothing more than that, I assure you. Do you remember much of anything?" He frowned, pulling his clipboard away from his side and holding a pen poised over the paper, waiting for my apparently important response.

"I don't remember a thing. Not a thing!"

That was it. The sobs burst from my throat and I covered my face with both hands. This wasn't a good time for a total breakdown, in front of this stranger.

He sighed. "I'm here to help you. You'll be just fine."

"Please," I said, so softly even I barely heard it. "Please tell me."

He took a deep breath.

"You were found late Tuesday morning by the river about four miles from here. Beaten and most likely left for dead. But obviously you're not dead, so that's one piece of good news."

Good news. I didn't want to hear the bad news. The river?

Dirt—lots of it—and blunt, repeated pain to my head and midsection.

I remember, "No, no, no!" and very little else.

I shook the thought aside and looked at the doctor again.

"What day is it now?"

"It's Thursday morning. We weren't sure what to think of your condition. Your friend hasn't left your side the whole time."

I looked around the room and saw no sign of Marty. My brain felt fuzzy again, as if the edges were smoldering from some lingering, untended fire.

"Marty's here? Where is he?"

"Oh," he laughed lightly. "He *was* here. And he'll be back. Bad timing, that's all. He went back to his hotel room to take a quick shower, change his clothes, and get some real food. It's the first time he's left since Tuesday."

Figures.

"I asked him if there was someone we could call for you, but he didn't know."

"No, he wouldn't know. We don't live anywhere near here. Or anywhere near each other." I sighed, frustrated and unsure how much detail he needed or what he already knew. "We were back in town for our class reunion. We're old friends. We both grew up here. We ... never mind."

The doctor nodded.

"My kids are with ... a friend ... back in Pittsburgh. Peter Bellows."

He didn't speak, apparently waiting for more details.

"I need to call Peter."

"Yes, of course. Write down names and numbers and I'll make sure that gets done for you."

"Where was I found?" It seemed the better part of wisdom to pursue the clinical, factual side of things first. I had a feeling there would be ample time to discover the gory details later.

"About four miles from here—down by the Delaware River near the Budget Inn. Along Route 611."

The Budget Inn. Marty. I remembered that part. The night of the reunion. He was mad at me. What did I do? Why was I outside the hotel? I couldn't remember. The fear washed back over me, and I tried to change the subject and shake it off.

"What exactly is wrong with me now?"

He consulted his chart, frowned a little, and took in a breath. "Multiple contusions on your torso, mostly along the right side of the body. Bruising and swelling on the left side of your face. You also have a very bad gash on your left calf—perhaps a knife wound."

I felt woozy for a moment.

A serrated kitchen knife runs along my left leg haphazardly, and adrenaline-enhanced pain rips into my flesh. "Lie still. . ."

"Are you all right, Miss Saunders?"

"What?" Dr. Bedside Manner looked at me intently, as if I were a lab animal. "It's Mrs. Saunders. I'm fine."

"You're awfully pale. Can I get you some water?"

I looked at the nightstand and saw a glass and a pitcher of water sitting there, far closer to me than to the doctor standing on the other side of the bed.

"No, thanks." I stared at the empty glass. "I'll be all right."

"Did you remember something?"

"Not really. Go on."

He cleared his throat and turned the page over on my chart. "You also have a badly sprained left ankle, which we think might have come from you running away rather than directly from the attack itself. Does this seem plausible?"

"I guess." Bursts of starry light shot into my field of vision ever so briefly, and I blinked them away. Dizzy.

I half-crawl, half-run down the side of the rocky, dirty slope, not seeing the rodent hole, and my foot wedges deep inside it. I cry out as it twists freakishly to the left.

"Miss Saunders, should I wait to continue?"

"Hmm? Umm, no. It's Mrs. Saunders. No, go ahead."

He coughed again, frowned a little more this time, and hesitated.

"What? What else is there?"

"We've sewn up the leg wound, but you may need a little physical therapy for the muscles it damaged."

The knife wound oozes thickening blood. I can feel it collecting on the side of my leg and then dribbling down my calf.

"I—said—lie—still!"

Where is my purse? Nowhere. Nowhere. He bends over me, his breath smelling of mint. His knee jabs my wounded calf and the pain blackens my sight for a brief moment.

God, tell me he isn't going to do this. What did they tell us to do in college? Lie still? Don't fight? It suddenly doesn't make sense, but I close my eyes and tell myself that it won't hurt too much and will all be over soon. I yowl without meaning to.

"Now you've gone and done it. This is all your fault."

He raises his arm far above me. I see his arm swoop down toward my head in an exaggerated arc. Quick, sharp pain, then dark.

"Miss Saunders, the nurse is giving you something to help you relax. It won't take long to kick in."

I felt tears on the side of my face but didn't remember crying them. "It's *Mrs.* Saunders. My husband died a few years ago. Just please find Marty."

He nodded silently. I wanted nothing more than to see a familiar face. *Marty, where are you?*

I didn't notice the nurse on the other side of the bed until she gripped my forearm tightly and twisted my arm just so, dabbing it quickly with an alcohol pad. Then the syringe was poised, the sting of the needle thrust under my skin and deep into the muscle of my arm. I winced and let a moan escape.

She swabbed the area again, flashed me a sympathetic smile, and quietly left the room with her instruments. *Marty ...*

I looked out the window, thinking it must be late morning or early afternoon. I closed my eyes, sighing, the weight of the world heavy on my chest.

My lip quivered shamelessly, my eyes salty and stinging with more tears. *Lord, tell me this isn't happening.*

The doctor must have sensed I needed reassurance. "You'll be fine. None of this is life-threatening, and none of it is even crippling. Just gashes and scrapes. We were concerned about the loss of consciousness there for a while, but you seem to have come out of the woods on that score. We'll be keeping an eye on you with the memory loss, but even that is fairly typical in a situation like this. Often it isn't permanent."

He smiled as he turned away from me, apparently thinking it would cheer me up to know that I'd continue to remember more details of what happened.

I wasn't so sure it would.

2

THE FUZZ IN MY BRAIN REFUSED TO DISSIPATE. I blinked hard at the light streaming in through the hospital window, but everything was still out of focus. With nothing familiar on which to anchor my thoughts, I was still disoriented as I sat up, trying to prop up pillows behind me without actually turning around. Until now stray movements had been too painful for me to start trying out new ones.

As I was reaching around behind me, punching down the top pillow to wedge it behind my back, I heard him. The blessed voice of Marty. Finally.

"You're awake. Thank God!"

Quickly rubbing my eyes, I gasped. "Marty? Is that you?" I knew it was him, but I couldn't yet focus to see him properly.

"Yes, it's me. I'm here. Do you have something in your eye?"

"You mean, besides my hands?"

He laughed. Such a good thing. His laugh felt comfortable, felt like home, and I couldn't help smiling when I heard it. I stopped rubbing my eyes and blinked hard, opening them fully. Like magic, there was Marty in front of me, smiling his little boy smile.

"Yeah, you'll be fine. Sense of humor seems intact."

He stood from his chair next to my bed and leaned in to hug me. In an unexplained knee-jerk reaction I stiffened momentarily, but it passed quickly and I hugged him back. His breathing caught in his throat as we hugged. I knew he was choking back quite a bit of pent-up emotion, God bless him. He'd been sitting here waiting for this moment for days.

We broke free and he backed down into the chair. I watched as his mousy gray-brown hair shifted forward and back with his own movements. I felt an urge to reach over and run my hand through it, to pull him close again.

"I guess they told you what happened, where they found you and everything, right?"

Marty spoke so cautiously, so delicately that I felt worse for him than I did for myself. He relaxed a little and crossed his lanky legs, one ankle on the other knee, then fiddled with his sneaker.

"More or less, yeah. Not sure how much of it I wanted to hear, or how much of it makes any sense right now. I'm just ... scared."

Marty sighed loudly and ran his own hand through his hair. "I know. I mean, I've been sitting here for days, pacing the floor. I was so worried you wouldn't be all right. They have no idea how that guy got into your hotel room in the first place."

I frowned, and Marty noticed it. "What? Is something coming back to you?"

"No, well, yes, well, *maybe*. I mean, I wasn't in my hotel room when it happened. That's *how* it happened."

"Where were you? You couldn't have been outside in the middle of the night on *purpose*. Not down by the Delaware."

I looked at him silently and blinked once or twice.

"You went down toward the river alone? We all assumed he'd *taken* you outside." I could almost hear his brain cells singeing around the edges as he tried to process this almost-unbelievable bit of information. "You were at the ... river? Alone?"

I blinked again. The memory was clearer now. I had gone outside sometime in the middle of the night, laden with little more than my hotel key, my purse, and the clothes I'd had on earlier in the afternoon. Suddenly it did seem like a stupid thing to do.

"Yeah, I think I was taking a walk near the river."

Marty stood up hastily, the chair skidding backwards from the force of his quick jump. He was obviously agitated, his hands flying around his head uncontrolled. "A woman out alone at night down there? You're crazy, right? Just tell me you're crazy." Now he was upset and scared, too.

"Marty, please ..."

He lowered his head and frowned. "Okay, I'm sorry. I don't mean to come down hard on you. Not now. Not fair. I'm sorry."

I sighed. He was doing what he always did. "Marty, stop it. This wasn't your fault. Stop groveling."

"I wasn't groveling, and yes, it was my fault. We both know it was my fault."

I knew no such thing. The memory of the earlier part of that night was becoming a little clearer, but I certainly didn't feel any sense of anxiety about Marty's involvement. Why was that?

"I don't see how my taking a walk is your fault."

He lowered his head into his hands.

"You obviously weren't just taking a walk. You must've forgotten what happened ... earlier."

"I didn't forget," I fibbed. "Honest."

"My guess is you wouldn't have had to *take* that walk if it wasn't for me."

"Stop it. Stop being so fatalistic. We've *talked* about this ..."

"This time it really is my fault. Think about it."

He was talking about something else, something I couldn't remember. "I am thinking about it. And I'm officially absolving you of all guilt."

I made an exaggerated sign of the cross between him and me. He tried to avoid smiling but failed.

"Thanks, Reverend Mother. Suddenly now we're both Catholics?"

I smiled in return.

"I don't *think* so!" we said in unison, chuckling together, friends again.

The gulf that still hung between us would have to be crossed at some point, but this didn't seem like the time to do it. After everything I'd been trying to process in the last few hours, making proper amends with Marty Emerson over some wrong I couldn't remember was way down low on my list. This temporary truce would have to do for now.

"Marty, could you do me a favor? I need to get in touch with Peter. I need to talk to him. The doctor said he'd have someone take care of that, but I don't know if he did."

"No problem. I have my cell phone in my car if you want to use that."

"Really? Yeah, that would work great. Would you mind?"

He stood up, exhaled comically, and shook his head exaggeratedly. "Hell yes, I mind! The nerve of you to go get beat up and then ask to use my *phone!*"

I broke out laughing a little too easily. He winked at me, relaxed his shoulders just a little, and headed for the door.

"I'll be right back. The car's just down in the lot outside your window there."

And with that he was out the door, and I was alone again. Alone. Story of my life. Alone with thoughts and memories I was now going to be forced to live for a second time. Memories of the past weekend and everything that landed me here in the first place. Suddenly I wished for the nurse and her accursed needle.

3

I SPENT MY PREPUBESCENT YEARS WORRYING about puberty, my adolescent years fretting over not being more popular with kids I hated anyway, and my early adulthood agonizing over death. Not about death specifically, but about dying. The thought of how I will get to the eternal side of life always held a morbid fascination for me. I often imagined it, against my will: Perhaps I'll be gunned down on the streets of Wilkinsburg one evening in front of the ATM across from the thrift store by some drug-crazed gang member who desperately needs the five dollars I just extracted from the machine to buy myself a Diet Pepsi and some Twinkies. Or maybe I'll contract some debilitating disease that'll bring prolonged, increasing pain as it progresses—one that's contagious, of course, isolating me from friends and relatives, even at the bitter end, when I die alone and penniless.

But I will never, ever simply pass away in my sleep. I was already convinced that even those who die in their sleep are jolted awake by some excruciating and horrible pain in their last moments but that they obviously haven't the forethought or presence of mind to scream or to leave anybody a detailed note describing their torture. So, the entire family forever believes that Grandma just peacefully fell asleep and never woke up.

It was with this healthy outlook that I now found myself in my thirties—widowed mother of two, finally beginning to accept God's providential hand in having brought me to this point. Granted, it was a struggle of immeasurable pain when it happened, like being trapped underwater, gulping painful bubbles of water down my throat, up my nose, someone's hand pushing my head deeper and deeper. But about six months ago, I seemed to resurface and click into a routine that made me feel normal for the first time since Jonathan died. I discovered that the drudgery of everyday existence was a godsend that kept me sane.

And just when I felt I was breathing freely again, last month God sent Marty, and worse, the mugger. And though the physical scars were healing fine, the nightmares continued. It was as if my subconscious was still trying to reconstruct the events I spent all day trying to keep forgotten. But by avoiding thoughts about the attack during the day, the ghastly event came back to haunt me while I slept. *When* I slept.

+ + + + +

I FELT MY SHOULDER BEING PINCHED AND SHAKEN and tried vainly to reconstruct reality without having to open my eyes.

"Mom—*Mom!*"

"What?" I grumbled half into my pillow, hoping my tone sounded sufficiently disapproving.

"Mom, are you waking up now?"

"What do *you* think, Faith?" I asked and winked one eye open. There she stood, her blonde hair unkempt, her front cowlick askew from being slept on for ten hours. "Is Mikey still sleeping?" I asked hopefully, knowing I could manage to hover here in a semi-conscious state for another half hour or so if he wasn't up yet.

"Nope. He's on the potty. He needs wiped."

Good morning, Emily. Welcome to the joys of motherhood. If you're not wiping one end, you're wiping the other.

"Needs *to be* wiped, Faith. Where do you think you're from, Pittsburgh?" I joked. She stood over me stoically.

"He needs *to be* wiped," she repeated flatly.

"Now? Is he done now?"

"Yeah."

I rolled over and off the bed, letting a guttural groan escape in protest of the early hour. So far no nausea this morning. I silently thanked God for small miracles, since the toilet was apparently *ocupado*.

"Sorry," Faith added, seeing my crusty countenance as well as my crusty eyes. The dream was gone with the morning. But it was bad sleep again last night, and this time for more reasons than one.

I leaned down to her, hugged her to me, and groaned again exaggeratedly as I squeezed. She smiled. "It's not your fault Mikey had to go to the bathroom, dope."

She grinned. "Okay, Mom. Is it Saturday?"

"Yeah, babe."

"Can I turn on cartoons?"

"Sure, go ahead down. Channel eleven, remember?"

"Yepper-yep. A one and a one next to it, eleven."

"That's right. Don't turn it up too loud, though."

"Okay," she said and bounded out of the room. I heard her feet dance down the steps as I plodded down the hall to the bathroom.

"Mikey, you done?" I called as I went, fully intending to pivot and head for the mattress again if he said no.

"Yeah, me done."

"*I'm* done, Mikey."

"No, *me* done, Mama," he corrected. He knew perfectly well which one of us was on the potty.

I went to the bathroom and peeked around the door. There he sat, perched atop the gaping moat of the toilet, suspending his bottom across the opening by locking his arms in place onto the edges of the seat, his bare feet dangling about six inches off the floor. His Spider-man underwear lay in a tiny bunch off to the side of the toilet.

"You need to be wiped, big guy?" I asked, hoping against hope that this would be the time he'd insist on doing it all by himself.

"Yeah," he answered, and, as delicately as he could manage, climbed off the potty. He unceremoniously bent over to make my task a tad easier, and talked to me upside down from between his legs.

"Faify down-tairs?"

"Yep. You gonna go down and watch cartoons with her?"

"Yeah! It 'toon day?"

"Yes it is, bud. Egg bread day too. You want some?"

"Yeah yeah!" he chanted. French toast was his favorite breakfast, and I only had time to make it on Saturdays. So, it was something I did faithfully, as much a part of the weekend as cartoons were on Saturday and worship was on the Lord's Day.

I helped him step into his underwear and pull them up, patted his butt playfully, and stood up. "Go ahead down, Mikey. Faith already has the TV on."

"Okay!" He scooted past me and out of the room.

"And make sure Faith doesn't have *Ren and Stimpy* on!" I called after him. "She should be watching channel one-one. Okay?"

"Yeah, one-one," he repeated, and his voice trailed off as he rounded the landing and headed the rest of the way down the steps. I was never sure just how much I expected Mikey to remember instructions like those, a bit too detailed and grown-up for him. But I issued them anyway, and the odds were about even that they would somehow be carried out. Often Faith would piece together Mikey's cryptic verbal messages and figure out on her own what I actually wanted. I had subconsciously maintained Jonathan's noble family tradition of always pressing the kids a little higher, letting them try that mental leap once in a while. He did it out of a finely honed sense of vision passed down from his own parents; I did it out of laziness.

I flushed the toilet and felt brave enough to examine my face closely in the mirror as I washed my hands while waiting for the water to stop running. I turned on the harsh fluorescent lights on either side of the mirror and subjected my eyelashes, eyebrows, and pores to intense scrutiny. It was by paying meticulous attention to the minutiae of my face that I avoided the big picture of remembering what had happened to me a few weeks earlier. Grunting, I inspected the small, greenish-yellow blotch of a stray bruise still visible on my left temple. I touched it gently and winced, hissing in breath and stiffening.

As I repeatedly tugged at my eyebrows with my thumb and forefinger, letting what few tiny hairs came loose fall into the sink, I heard the phone in the bedroom ring. I nearly poked myself in the eye and blinked two or three times as I straightened and turned.

My feet found their customary nine lengthened steps to the phone, and I picked up the receiver and cleared my throat at the same time.

"Hello-Saunders," I answered, as I had done for so long that it had become one word.

"Emily? Hi. Good morning."

"Oh, hi, Pete. How are you?"

"Just fine. We still on for today?" he asked.

The psalm-sing. I had completely forgotten about it. "Is that today?"

"Yes. Do you still want to go? Did you forget?"

"No, I didn't forget," I fibbed. "But it slipped in and out of my mind most of the day yesterday. What time do we have to be in Beaver Falls?"

"Four o'clock."

"Hmm," I calculated aloud, "that means we should leave no later than two or two-fifteen, allowing for traffic out near the airport. Sound right?"

"Yeah, I was figuring I'd get over to your place by two, so we can get the kids settled in the car and then be on the road by two-fifteen."

"Sounds perfect," I said, referring to his calculations and not necessarily the prospect of the day itself.

"Okay then, so I'll see you at two?"

"Great. See you then," I confirmed.

"Okay, Emily. See ya then. Bye."

I put the receiver down before I heard it click on his end. I was afraid if I didn't, he'd say something else. I stood there next to the dresser in a fog, not quite sure if I sounded too clipped. I felt guilty. There was absolutely nothing wrong with Peter Bellows. Not a thing. And in the past three months, believe me, I had tried to find something.

Were we dating? Not really. Were we "seeing" each other? Perhaps. We made the mistake of sitting next to each other in church two Sundays in a row recently, which meant we might as well be engaged as far as most of the congregation was concerned. Pete had even held Mikey on his lap during much of the sermon last week, thereby sealing our public relationship even further. At the time, it just seemed like a good way to keep Mikey quiet.

I should have known better, because frankly, I wasn't ready to be the topic of conversation again. I was just becoming content with going about my petty little business of daily survival all over again, not having to talk through everything with well-meaning friends who thought I needed to *let it out, Emily, just let it out*. I was sick and tired of wearing my heart on my sleeve. I needed the sleeve space for more important things, like the saliva of a toddler who's fallen asleep on my shoulder. I learned the hard way in the past few years that yes, talk is cheap. And, God be praised, silence is golden. It was in the silence, even in the thick smothering silence of the dead of night, that I could hear God. That still, small voice never seemed smaller, or paradoxically, clearer, as in those times at the end of the day after the kids were asleep, and the TV was off, and the entire world finally shut up and left me alone.

The prayers at those times were fast and furious and almost Pentecostal in nature. I sometimes wondered if Jonathan would find them ironically amusing or desperately sad. I just ran off at the mouth, mixing extemporaneous soliloquies with the Lord's Prayer, or questions from the Catechism, or snatches of the psalter, half sung, half chanted. As often as not, I would sob myself out of prayer and into a

fitful sleep and wake up in the morning with heartburn and a throbbing headache. But I was rarely as aware of God's presence as through
those lonely hours. And these days I was learning a lesson: His presence is comforting. A lesson I apparently needed to learn anew after
these past few weeks.

I stood there next to my dresser, staring at the phone, until I heard
Faith close the bathroom door down the hall. I walked past the bathroom and padded down the steps. Rounding the corner out of the dining room and into the kitchen, I heard the Care Bears arguing about
something from the living room, and the relative silence in the room
told me that Mikey was probably sitting cross-legged about two feet
from the TV, eyes glued to the screen, mouth slightly open. I would
be able to slip into the basement unnoticed and take that load of wet
clothes from last night out of the washer and put them into the dryer.

After a quick glance through the dining room and into the living
room to be sure Mikey wasn't on his way out to see me, I opened the
basement door, switched on the light, and tiptoed down the steps.
The cold musty air assaulted my nose and I drew in a breath. Opening
the lid of the washer at the foot of the stairs, I leaned over the barrel
and sniffed. *Good, I don't have to re-rinse them.* An armful of cold wet
laundry came free from inside the washer, and I methodically turned
forty-five degrees to drop the bundle on top of the dryer. Three more
bundles followed and the washer was empty. The glass door swung
open and I transferred the heavy clothes from the top of the dryer
to the inside. Crouching down and retrieving the stray sock that fell
out of my clutches and hit the dusty concrete floor, I smacked it once
against my thigh and tossed it into the dryer.

With a quick slam of the door, I straightened and lifted the lint
trap out of the lid, rolling back the thick layer of gray-blue lint,
dumping it into the garbage bucket next to the dryer. Tiny particles of
sweet-smelling lint poofed out of the bucket and floated back down.
After replacing the trap I turned the timer to fifty minutes, high heat.
The dryer whirred into life and the load began to tumble and thud
inside in an uneven but steady rhythm.

I bent down again and peered through the glass door to watch the clothes gyrate to their own beat. My oldest pair of jeans danced around in the front of the load, and I watched with unusual fascination as they somersaulted in crowded gymnastics. On some turns they seemed to ball themselves up in an effort to fend off the moisture-draining heat; on others they unfurled, hid behind other pieces of clothing, and skipped around the outside edges of the dryer in a defiant prance.

Catch me if you can ...

A lump rose uninvited into my throat as I saw myself in a similarly threadbare pair of jeans, lurching and stumbling through the rotating Barrel-O-Laffs in the Fun House at Norris Fun Park in Easton. I felt the hair on the back of my neck prickle up as the emotional upheaval of a muggy August night came cascading back to me all at once. All seven of us sitting on a pair of wet, dilapidated park benches next to the Mouse, a single-car roller coaster that had been shut down years earlier. Rumor had it that one day a young boy had been paralyzed when his car had run off its track around the far curve and had plummeted him to the patchy grass beneath. We all sat there exchanging stupid, sick jokes about the contraption, with the haunting music of the carousel melting over us from across the park. At one point we had all stopped speaking, all fumbled for something to say next, and had all drawn blanks.

It had been drizzling off and on all evening, but since we'd been planning this big blow-out for weeks, we decided to see it through. We couldn't reschedule it; Marty was trekking off to Northwestern come sun-up. The evening was supposed to have been our last fling together as a group before we all went off to college and grew up.

We started out the evening with some skating in the roller rink inside the park, next to the Whip, just over the one-lane bridge spanning Norris Creek. Roller skating was the most universal "sport" among Easton kids while we were all growing up. We met just inside the door at the front desk, where we each paid for two hours of skat-

ing and stated our shoe size, loudly, to Ma Long, the sole proprietor
of the rink since 1956 when her husband had died. By the time we
were on the brink of starting our own lives, Ma Long's park had already begun teetering on the edge of becoming a health hazard. The
roller rink itself had held up better than most of the park, but it only
made money on children's birthday parties on Saturday afternoons, a
fine and long-standing tradition of elementary school Easton kids for
decades. The turnout on an Open Skate night in the middle of the
week was less than dramatic. These days, everyone made the trip up to
Allentown to skate in the new rink.

I watched the sparse group of skaters make their way almost le-
thargically around and around the oval rink as I waited for Ma Long
to shuffle back from the shelves with my size 6 white skates. Todd,
Matt, and Hannah had already gotten their skates and were walking down the corridor next to the rink to the benches to put them
on. Marty was directly behind me, and tapped me on the shoulder. I
leaned my head back a bit, eyes still fixed on the mesmerizing, herd-
instinct swaying of the skaters on the floor.

"Hmm?"

"How much ya wanna bet they still don't have my size?"

I laughed, took my skates from Ma Long, who looked quite distracted by the mugginess, and headed down the corridor. In a while,
Marty, Hank, and Jill followed me, and we sat all in a row, bent over
double, fussing with our skates.

The familiar smell of ancient, worn shoe leather wafted into our
noses as we laced them up. For as often as we had all been here as kids,
it was surprising that none of us owned our own pair of skates. Then
again, no Easton kid owned his own skates—at every skating party,
everyone used the rink's prehistoric ones.

This time I was fortunate. I got a pair equipped not only with
rubber stoppers on the fronts but also with little metal hooks where
the shoelace eyelets should have been. I was the first to have my skates
laced fully, and as snugly as I dared without cutting off my circulation.
I hopped out of my chair and whirled around.

"Well, what's the matter, slow pokes?"

Hannah continued to lace frantically, but looked up enough to see my skates.

"Oh, no fair, you cheated," she grunted, yanking long ends of frayed shoelace through unwilling eyelets. "Shit! Whaddya call those little tab things on the ends of shoelaces? I don't have any on mine!"

"Iglets," Todd offered, almost finished lacing his size 12 black skates.

"No, no, no," Marty huffed. "Not iglets—*aglets*. They're aglets." To the casual observer, Marty might have seemed annoyed at Todd, but we all knew that what really had him miffed were his skates. The rink had always been short of skates Marty's size during all our years together, even as Marty's feet grew. It was almost uncanny. Tonight, he was stuffing his size 11 feet into size 10½ skates.

"Geez, I hate these things. Band-Aids or not, it'll be blisters tomorrow on the trip."

Todd finished double-knotting his laces and stood up. "Ah, shut up, ya crybaby." He grinned. And off he whirred onto the skating floor. "C'mon, Emily!"

I followed, grateful for some familiar company on the nearly barren hardwood floor of the rink. "Hey, Todd," I said, as I glided up alongside him on the first turn. "When are you leaving?"

"Next Wednesday, first thing in the morning. My folks are renting a little trailer."

"Mine, too, even with the pickup. I think I might've overpacked."

"What are you bringing?"

"A better question is, what am I *not* bringing?"

"I'd hate to be your roommate. When are you leaving?"

"A week from today. I think I'm the last one."

"Nope, Matt's not starting for almost two weeks."

"Yeah, but he's not moving anywhere. He's commuting. He doesn't count."

Matt and Hannah skated past us in rapid succession. Hannah grabbed my arm as she passed in an obvious effort to pry me away from Todd. I giggled and let her momentum pull me slightly in front of him. At Hannah's signal, we cut him off and zipped into the center of the rink, away from what little flow of traffic there was. She huddled near me and spoke lowly into my ear.

"What do you think?"

"What?" I asked, my ear bent next to her lips, eager for the dirt.

"Before Jill gets out here, what do you think of her and Marty?"

"What about her and Marty?"

"Well, you know. The way he looks at her."

I tried not to sound emotionally uprooted by this statement.

"What do you mean, 'the way he looks at her'?"

"You know," she said knowingly, nudging me in the side with her elbow. It hurt, and not just physically. "God, he fawns all over her."

"He does not."

"Look," she said, grabbing my arm again and twisting me around to look at the two of them, still on the benches lacing their skates. Hank had just skated onto the rink, so they were alone. I saw Jill busily fiddling with Marty's right skate, chattering away, Marty red-faced and smiling. I looked away and turned back to Hannah.

"So she's helping him lace his skates? Did you see the pair they gave him this time? They were so frayed—"

"Emily, you don't have to defend him or anything. They're allowed to like each other."

"Yeah, but not *that* way," I blurted and felt my face immediately flush. Hannah gave me an inquiring sideways look. "I mean, she's not even his type."

Hannah began to skate slowly, and I kept up with her. "No, but male hormones aren't all that picky about stuff like that, Em." She laughed. I just smiled a little, skating along on autopilot, and followed Hannah out from the middle of the rink and back onto the main drag.

"Besides," she continued, "he was talking to her about a lot of stuff. She seemed interested too. Who knows?"

Hannah's interest in the whole topic seemed to be flagging. I, on the other hand, was just beginning to get acutely interested.

"When was he talking to her about ... stuff?" I asked loudly, as Hannah began to pull ahead of me.

"Shhh," she said, turning around and throwing her glance behind me. I whipped my head around in time to see Marty wheeling up behind me fast. "In A.P. Bio right before graduation," she answered, and sped out in front of me. As if on cue, Marty appeared at my side in Hannah's place.

"Howdy, little lady," he said, and grabbed me around the waist in an effort to slow himself down to my pace. I jerked unsteadily forward for a moment, one skate coming involuntarily off the floor, and then regained my balance.

"Whoa, hi," I giggled, flailing my arms just a little.

"What about A.P. Bio?" Marty asked innocently. He probably couldn't imagine a conversation involving me and the term "A.P. Bio." I had set a school precedent by opting out of my last two years of science entirely, in favor of English electives.

"Well," I said, smiling weakly. "Hannah said you used to bother Jill about stuff in A.P. Bio. True?"

"Yep," he offered simply. "Oh, wait! Listen!"

I trained my ears on the world around me, looking upward as people always do when they're listening for something. All I heard was the low buzz of a dozen or so conversations, the *rrrrrd-rrrrrdd-rrrrrrr* of old rubber wheels on older wooden floors, and the PA system blaring out a scratchy, distorted version of Marie Osmond gushing her way through "Paper Roses."

Marty's hands moved up to my shoulders, and he nestled his chin on my shoulder from behind. "It's...it's...it's...*Marie!*" he breathed into my ear. I guffawed, spitting out a hearty laugh.

"Shhhh—we'll have to finish this conversation later. I'm enraptured!"

"Aw, c'mon. You know Ma Long'll play it again in twenty minutes."

"Yeah, right after 'Build Me Up, Buttercup,' and what're the other ones?"

"Umm, 'Sugar, Sugar' ..."

"Yeah!"

"Oh, and 'Soldier Boy'!"

"Yeah!" he yelled again, letting go of my shoulder and clapping his hands over his heart, scooting a bit ahead of me and spinning around to face me, skating backwards.

"Sollldier boy! Oh, my little sollldier boy! I'll—be—true—to—you!" he crooned over Marie's sapping strains. Marty held out his hands, still skating backwards effortlessly, pushing himself forward with his heels. I grinned and grabbed his hands, falling into his swaying motion as he continued the song.

"You were my firrrrst love...." He nodded to me in rhythm, signaling my turn to sing.

"And you'll be my laassst love...." I nodded back.

Just as Marty opened his mouth to sing the next line, Hank came up right behind me and jabbed his kneecaps into the backs of my knees. My legs wobbled and involuntarily buckled, and I bounced hard onto the floor, biting my lip as I hit. As I went down, I let go of Marty's hands, but he clutched back at mine in a vain effort to keep me from hitting the floor. As I sat sprawled on the rink floor, legs spread in oh-so-unladylike a fashion, Marty bent down in front of me, still holding my hands.

"You okay?" he asked, wincing himself as he saw the drops of blood welling up on my rapidly swelling lip.

"Yeah, okay, I s'pose," I said, and pulled both my lips in on themselves to hide the damage.

Hank had stopped as well and looked down sheepishly at us. "Em, I'm sorry. I thought you might wiggle a little, but I didn't think you'd fall."

"What kind of man are you?" Marty chimed in. I patted him on the knee and shook my head.

"S'okay, really. Just help me up."

Marty pulled me to my feet, a bit more chivalrously than I was used to, even from Marty.

Todd put in an obligatory appearance to see how I was the next time he skated past, and then grinned at Hank for his deft move. I saw Marty glare at him, and I wondered suddenly how often they had been pitted against each other. Both Marty and I had our moral sensibilities easily offended, but I realized that a group of teenage boys would be more apt to stir his ire than a circle of girls would be to stir mine.

Jill and Hannah approached one at a time, and with the presence of the entire Clique, the tension fizzled out. Now even Marty could not hang on to his anger at such ungentlemanly behavior. It had been a joke, and even though it had resulted in the misfortune of a friend (a girl, yet!), it had still been intended as a prank. Besides, except for a fat lip and probably a bruised tailbone, I was fine. I began to skate on, as if nothing embarrassing had just happened, and Jill and Hannah clipped themselves onto either side of me. Only Marty was left hovering at the scene of the crime. I looked behind me, Marty shrugged, and I heard "Soldier Boy" come rasping through the corner speaker as we passed. Marty grinned and blew me a kiss, then started to skate again.

+ + + + +

AFTER ONLY AN HOUR IN THE RINK, we left to hit other points of interest (and nostalgia, if the truth be told) before the park closed. We handed in our skates and waited as Marty bandaged up his right foot with toilet paper to cushion the blisters before putting his sneakers back on.

It was still drizzling off and on, not enough to close the park, but enough to make the older rides rattle and squawk. Despite the odd encounter in the rink, and the dreariness of the weather, we all maintained an acceptable level of cheeriness through the Pretzel, the bumper cars, and the Fun House, all of which we had to ourselves. Inside the Fun House, we all shoved our way into the revolving Barrel-O-Laffs at the same time and spent a full ten minutes pitching left and right, toppling over one another and laughing ourselves breath-less. When Hank hooked his tank top on a splintering piece of wood on the side of the barrel and drew blood from his shoulder, it was all Marty could do to keep himself from feeling a perverse sense of jus-tice. I could see it in his eyes. And, in spite of myself, I liked seeing that in him.

We all moved on to the less daring Room of Mirrors. In one of the wide-angle mirrors, I inadvertently got an accurate view of myself in fifteen years after three sit-down jobs and two pregnancies. Even then, instinctively, the sight depressed me, and I led the troops elsewhere.

On the two-story, indoor wooden sliding board in the adjoining room, Hank and Matt persisted in annoying us girls by sliding down immediately after us, trying to prod and cajole us into sliding faster. Our shrill squeals echoed inside the lofted, deserted structure. This room was the one place in the park where we couldn't make out the strains of the merry-go-round, and it seemed deathly quiet when we all stopped sliding and headed for the exit. Hank had found another splinter on his last trip down, and he wasn't having fun anymore. We didn't let him forget it.

Next we awakened a ride attendant from a boredom-induced half doze to run the Whip for us. He sat on his stool, methodically scratch-ing his sparsely haired head, while we split up and crowded into two of the six army-green cars, and he watched us, still bored and still half asleep.

After our painfully silent stint on the Whip, barely worth the two tickets we had each forked over, we were left with the carousel. We let the drifting music draw us the rest of the way across the park where it stood, majestically overlooking the nearly empty parking lot. It was fully lit around its dome with scores of high-wattage clear bulbs, all blinking somewhat out of kilter with the beat of the chiming, absurd-ly cheery circus music issuing from its belly. While we were still a few dozen feet away, it beckoned fetchingly, a melancholy sight with its menagerie of fifty-plus animals, from the obligatory horses to scaled-down giraffes and overgrown jackrabbits.

We jumped on as the carousel was beginning a new song, and spread ourselves out evenly around the circle, barely able to see the friends on either side of us. In front of me I saw Jill churning up and down on one of the hand-carved lions, talking loudly to Todd in front of her. I was astride a stationary light brown horse and turned to see Marty behind me, standing on the warped wooden floor of the merry-go-round, clutching one of the vertical bars and leaning way outside the actual parameter of the ride. As we passed the free-standing ticket booth inside the carousel pavilion, Marty reached out as far and as precisely as he could, screwed up his face, and plucked a single metal ring out of the jutting feeder arm. He grinned and held the ring aloft for me to admire, and I paid him back with a smile of my own and a thumbs-up sign. He tried to show off the next two times around, and missed both times, whacking his wrist on the end of the feeder the second time. He winced, walked himself up to me pole by pole, and climbed onto the pumping rabbit next to me when it was at its nadir.

"Well, it's better than I've ever done," I comforted, bobbing my head slowly to follow his oscillating gaze.

"You can't even reach the rings!"

I nodded and grinned. "I know."

He cocked back a thumb and fired an imaginary finger-pistol shot into my forehead, then blew the smoke from his index finger. He twirled the illusory gun and returned it to its holster. "C'mere, pilgrim," he summoned in his best John Wayne, scooting forward and patting the saddle behind him.

I met his gaze, half-closed my eyes suspiciously, and said, "I didn't know the Duke rode a bunny."

Marty looked down at the frozen rabbit underneath him, its legs outstretched in a permanent and powerful rigor mortis hop. "Oh, uh, well," he improvised, "this old thing? I musta left my horse back home in my other pants." He executed a clumsy dismount from high in the air and sat behind me on my motionless horse. "There. You happy, Miss Smarty Pants?" he asked me.

"Yeah," I said, and I realized as we came around again to a panoramic view of the deserted parking lot that it was one of the biggest fibs I had ever told in my short life.

+ + + + +

THE CLOTHES TRIPPED AND FELL INTO A WAD onto the side of the dryer and were carried around by the centrifugal force.

Lie still ...

Suddenly there was thick silence, and I saw the laundry laying limp at the bottom of the dryer. The manufactured scent of the softener sheet emerged, and I realized I must have been sitting on the filthy concrete, staring at the dryer for the entire fifty-minute cycle.

I said, lie still ...

My stomach staggered, and suddenly I was bounding up the steps, through the kitchen, rounding the corner of the living room, and taking the stairs to the second floor at breakneck speed.

A minute later, as I wiped the corner of my mouth and flushed the toilet, I doubted I'd be making French toast after all.

4

I WOKE UP SUFFOCATING IN BLACKNESS and sat bolt upright in my bed. I wasn't going to sweat this one away; I was already sweating like a pig and my heart raced furiously under my skin. And I certainly wasn't going to will it away; things had gone way beyond that in the month since I returned home from the hospital in Easton. I toyed with the idea of praying it away, but a good Calvinist never puts much faith in such blatant God-manipulation. Besides, it never really worked for very long. And that, after all, is what mattered at 4 a.m. in the hazy three-quarters darkness of my room. It still ran guilt streaks coursing ice blue through my veins to think that, when push came to shove, I'd go sniveling and groveling to God much the same way a penniless addict went to his pusher.

Yet, once more here I sat in a sleeper's gallery watching it all, a lone ticket holder at my own strangling nightmare. Again I hadn't seen the man's face—I just heard his rage—before I was plunged first into a gray oblivion and then back into my bed, sitting up, bathed in sweat, heart racing. Tonight I was reduced to the only practical solution left to a converted Covenanter like me, awake at such an ungodly hour: television.

I swung my legs out from under the blanket and over the side of the bed, fumbling my way to the bathroom. So much of my life revolved around the bathroom lately that I momentarily considered moving a couch and desk in there for convenience. By the time the light was on and my underpants were around my ankles, I was fully awake.

"What am I doing? I don't even have to go." I hiked my pants back up under my long T-shirt and turned to look at myself in the mirror.

I shut my eyes to the sight that greeted me. "Why do I look at myself in this thing?"

No one answered. The house was still. The very peace and quiet I craved and longed for all day was the very thing that haunted me in the middle of the night.

"Be careful what you wish for, Emily," I said, opening my eyes again in spite of myself. "You just might get it."

For a moment I wasn't looking at my own reflection but at a wholly different person. She had no name, no particular age, no personality. She existed inside the flat world of the mirror, survived there day to day, but had no purpose.

"Why am I awake?" I asked her. She looked as perplexed as I did. "Hmmph. You're no help." I stepped away from the mirror and she instantly disappeared out of my world, content to retreat silently into her own.

I switched the light back off on my way out of the bathroom, plunging myself into darkness again. I shuffled to the kids' room, clicking open the door as quietly as I could. The soft, pleasant glow of the Gumby night-light beckoned me inside. I heard Mikey's breathing from the doorway. *He's gonna be a snorer, just like his dad.* I walked over to him lying peacefully on the bottom bunk, and bent to sit on the edge of the bed. After pushing the hair off his damp forehead where it had been plastered by perspiration, I yanked the sheet off his torso. He sighed, turned over to face the wall, and sunk back into the nether regions of sleep.

Sleep was Mikey's friend. He never fought it, never cried at bed-time. He accepted it as a welcome end to a happy and tiring day. I envied him. For me, sleep was an elusive and slippery creature with no substance. When I did grab it and catch it, I was often disappointed in its performance. It never satisfied, never did much more than frustrate and tire me more than when I was chasing it.

I stood upright to reach the top bunk and kissed Faith lightly on the forehead. She was leaning smack up against the rail of the bunk, so I slowly pushed her back toward the middle a little. She didn't miss a breath. Faith hated going to bed and whined at every opportunity about the injustice of a forced bedtime. But once she fell asleep, she slept like a log. She was just like I was when I was a kid. How could I explain to a four-year-old what a blessing a good night's sleep can be?

I turned away from my children and tiptoed to the door. "Good-bye, Gumby," I said, and shut the door slowly.

I padded down the steps, rounded the corner into the living room, and swiped the remote control off the top of the converter box on my way past the TV to the couch. *Converter box*, I thought, as I sunk wearily into the overstuffed cushions. *If only it were that simple for everyone. Click, you're saved. Click, temptation's gone.* I realized what a trite statement that was, but nevertheless enjoyed claiming it as my own. At 4 a.m. all my thoughts are brilliant.

After an eternity of flipping through half-hour commercials for weight-lifting equipment, diet pills, and miracle cures for baldness, I decided to risk another nightmare and went back upstairs.

Once back in my room, I turned on the light and climbed into the middle of the bed. I saw the test strip still sitting on my vanity and fought the urge to get it and sit up the rest of the night gawking at its bright red plus sign. I sighed audibly, feeling the anxiety and confu-sion fighting to get to the surface again.

+ + + + +

THE RUSH-HOUR TRAFFIC EARLIER THAT SAME DAY had been light. Faith and Mikey dawdled a little less than usual when I picked them up from Cassie's house after work. They held off whining about dinner; things went relatively swimmingly. The first half of the trip home was blissfully quiet.

"Mommy?" Faith piped up suddenly from the back seat.

"Yeah, honey?" I shouted into the windshield, keeping my eyes dutifully forward.

"Can we get a Happy Meal tonight?"

"No—" I began firmly, but I was drowned out by the piercing harmonized descant of Mikey directly behind me.

"Yeah! M'Donald's! M'Donald's! Yeah!"

"No!" I repeated, smacking the steering wheel for emphasis. "I don't get paid till next Tuesday. Don't even think about it."

"Mom, you said we could get a Happy Meal again. You did."

"Faith, I didn't say *when* we'd do it again. You can't do it without money, hon."

"M'Donald's! Hap' Meal!" Mikey continued to chant, and I felt the back of my seat move rhythmically.

"Mikey, get your feet off the back of my seat—now!"

The seat-pushing ceased, accompanied by a disgruntled noise from Mikey. With my peripheral vision, I saw the small pharmacy bag peeking out from my unzipped purse on the passenger's seat. Mikey's defiance seemed insignificant. McDonald's would have been simpler, but I honestly didn't have the money. I'd have to dream up something for dinner again. *Living hand to mouth takes up a lot of my head*, I thought.

I reached over and grabbed a tissue out of my purse while I was waiting at a red light, quickly dabbing my eyes and blowing my nose. As I was trying to put the tissue into the small garbage bag tied onto the radio knob, the car behind me blared its horn. The light had turned green.

"All right, all right, buddy," I answered, again into the windshield, and pulled into the intersection.

"Why are you talking to that man, Mom?"

"Faith, never mind. He was just rude to me, that's all."

"Green means go. You go when it's green."

"Faith," I said curtly, "don't tell me what to do. Don't be a back-seat driver."

She was silent for the remainder of the trip, and I pulled up to the house in the middle of a mental argument with myself about the merits of taking the test before starting dinner. I unbuckled my seat belt, grabbed my purse, and slipped out of the car. I flipped the seat forward and saw Mikey, sound asleep in his car seat, head wedged up against the side. I sighed, undid his seat belt, and scooped him up in my arms.

"Faith, climb out this side too, please," I instructed quietly. She complied, and we walked in peace to the side door of the house.

"Here, Momma." She found the marked house key in the front of my purse slung over my shoulder and unlocked the door for me. I carried Mikey inside and walked directly into the living room, leaning over slightly so that he slid onto the couch, changing breathing patterns for a moment but still sleeping. I straightened, sighed, and turned to head back to the kitchen.

Faith was in the kitchen holding the bag from the pharmacy in her hand. She had taken it out of my purse when she grabbed the key.

"Faith, give that back. It's not yours," I said calmly through clenched teeth.

"Mommy, did you buy me something?"

"No, honey, I didn't. It's something for me." I balked. "Medicine."

"Are you sick again?"

"No, not really."

"You sure do get sick a lot."

"I know. Now, can I have the bag back, please?"

I frowned as menacingly as I could without looking downright mean.

"Okay," she said, suddenly uninterested. "Here," she added, and gave me the bag. I took it with a bit more of a snap of my wrist than I needed to.

"Thanks, dear. Hey, why don't you go see if *SpongeBob* is still on?"

She was a bright girl and understood a gentle prod when she heard one. "Sure, Mom. Do you want Mikey to keep sleeping?"

"Yeah, at least until I get dinner going."

She left the room, and I was alone with the bag. I walked out of the kitchen and climbed the steps just off the living room. Feeling instinctively secretive, I walked into the spare bedroom I used as a study and shut the door behind me. I clutched the bag against my chest, closed my eyes, and took a deep breath before opening it. Hands shaking, I fumbled with the test kit inside and it came out of the bag, missing the nervous grasp of my other hand and falling onto the floor.

Worried that Faith would barge in, see the kit on the floor, and ask more probing questions, I stooped hastily and swiped the small box off the floor where it had landed at my feet. The box came open easily, and I took out the instruction sheet and long plastic cylinder. It reminded me of a digital thermometer—white, slender, smooth—but this wasn't a thermometer. You don't pee on a thermometer. At least I sure didn't.

I couldn't very well do this in the study, so I took everything—box, bag, receipt, tester, instruction sheet—into the adjoining bathroom. Taking the tester in my right hand, I let the other items fall haphazardly into the sink. Before I could change my mind, I remembered that the faucet had been leaking again the past few days. The flimsy instruction sheet landed right smack in the middle of a small, wet puddle that had collected in the bottom of the sink and immediately began to soak up water like it was a sponge and not a piece of paper.

"Shit," I said without thinking. I snatched the tissue-thin sheet and held it aloft, up out of the water. Too late. It had already begun to dissolve and tear itself asunder right up the middle, making the crucial English portion of the instructions virtually useless. Naturally, the French instructions were intact. I hadn't taken French since sixth grade. All I remembered from that fiasco of a class was that *serviette* meant "napkin." I doubted that was going to be much help.

"I just did this a few years ago. Can't be that hard to remember how to pee on the end of a stick."

Thus convinced, I locked the bathroom door and set to work. The procedure itself was quite simple, albeit genuinely unladylike and awkward. The tough part was not peeing all over my hand in the process. And I had apparently given myself another opportunity to prove just how tough it is.

"Yuck."

With the now-wet tester balanced carefully on the edge of the sink, I cleaned myself up, put all my lower clothing back in its proper place, and washed my hands. From what I remembered, these things only took about three or four minutes to register an accurate result. By the time I was done scrubbing my arms up to the elbows and drying them off, I had used up half that time already.

I put the lid down and sat, waiting for the slow minutes to pass, not daring to look at the strip too early for fear of jinxing it. Suddenly I believed in jinxes and superstitions. I felt queasy and ill, much the same as I had every morning for the last week.

My hands held my chin up as my elbows rested on my knees. Bent over like this, I looked down at the floor, with nothing else to do but await the black hole of doom that I felt closing in on me. After what seemed to be days, but was really no more than five minutes, I stood on wobbly legs and peered straight down at the test strip still perched on the side of the sink. Staring back at me was a thick, bright red, clear-as-day plus sign.

Bile and adrenaline surged through my body, each fighting for supremacy. In a panic I turned back to the toilet, lifted the lid, dropped to my knees on the cold hard tile, and vomited violently into the bowl that I forgot to flush only five minutes earlier.

"Oh, Lord, please, no ..." I groaned as my stomach continued to evict everything residing in it since lunchtime.

5

AS I HAD DONE NEARLY A THOUSAND TIMES BEFORE, I stepped across the threshold of Calvin Presbyterian Church. The same familiar tile welcomed my old shoes; the same coat rack dangled its matching plastic coat hangers at me as I walked past, Mikey in my arms, grasping Faith's small hand tightly, eyes forward.

"Hi, Emily," came to me from warm friends, passing acquaintances, and other blissfully ignorant church members, many of whom had prayed for me right after my attack last month. I nodded, smiled, and kept on walking, afraid of their eyes, their smiles, any of their questions beyond "How are you?" Mercifully, I heard little more than the perfunctory hellos common among the hurrying, habitually late arrivals. I rounded the short corner into the sanctuary, furtively glancing around for an empty half a pew to fit the children and me. There was one with enough space on the side aisle along the right-hand side of the room, but I would have to walk up beyond nearly a dozen rows of quiet, settled people to get to it. It was, though, my only hope of refuge during the hour and a half of worship time coming up. Whether or not I would be able to dodge those twelve pews of people while beating my hasty retreat afterwards was a different story.

Faith and I shuffled along the side aisle and ducked into the empty pew, where I let Mikey slide off my hip and onto the bench next to me. Stealing a quick shot around me I saw Peter sitting far off on the left side of the sanctuary, with enough space reserved on either side of him for me and the kids. He had been expecting us to sit with him, again. That was another bridge I'd have to cross at some point. No hurry, though. *Delay that one as long as possible*, I thought.

I barely had time to gather my thoughts and plan my escape route before our pastor, Ray Compton, stood up from behind the pulpit and cleared his throat. He placed himself comfortably behind the lectern, swiped a stray lock of hair off his forehead deftly, and adjusted the microphone a tad before speaking.

"The call to worship this morning is from Psalm 13. Listen to God's Word: 'How long, O Lord? Will You forget me forever? How long will You hide Your face from me? How long shall I take counsel in my soul, Having sorrow in my heart daily? How long will my enemy be exalted over me? Consider and hear me, O Lord my God; Enlighten my eyes, Lest I sleep the sleep of death; Lest my enemy say, "I have prevailed against him"; Lest those who trouble me rejoice when I am moved. But I have trusted in Your mercy; My heart shall rejoice in Your salvation. I will sing to the Lord, Because He has dealt bountifully with me.'"

Mikey yawned from his spot up against me, and I tousled his hair with one hand, throwing my other arm around Faith. Giving myself permission to relax a little, I turned my attention to Pastor Ray.

"Let's stand and sing Psalm 116A from *The Book of Psalms for Worship*." He held his psalter aloft in his left hand and motioned for the congregation to rise with his right. We complied, psalters dutifully open to 116A. Everett Newman, our precentor, stood and pulled his pitch pipe from his front pants pocket, blowing a B-flat softly to give himself the proper starting pitch of the chord. His spiral-bound psalter was perched in his left hand, and he intoned each note of the B-flat chord loudly for all of us to hear, ending with the opening pitch of Psalm 116A. Not that any of us could tell a B-flat from a beehive.

How fervently I love the LORD *– My cries for help He hears!*
So, all my life I'll call on Him Who turned to me His ear.
The ropes of death entangled me And wrapped themselves around;
The terrors of the grave took hold – I grief and trouble found.

Everett's right arm struck firmly with each beat of the 4/4 mea-
sures. What our singing lacked in feeling he more than made up for
in his leading. In our shrinking, aging congregation only Everett
possessed enough singing ability to keep from embarrassing himself.
Everett's prolific musical talents were certainly wasted among the
tone-deaf members of Calvin Church. Even a blue-blood Covenanter
might have wished for musical instruments in worship to drown out
Daisy Henderson's feeble attempts at the highest soprano notes and
Alan Ward's bench-rumbling bad bass. The rest of us stumbled around
somewhere between the two of them, watching notes on the psalter's
pages go up and down and trying to make our weak voices at least
match the general direction of the notes.

Upon the LORD*'s name then I called, In my extremity:*
"O LORD*, I beg You, spare my life; And let my soul go free."*
The LORD *our God is kind and just; Compassionate is He.*
The LORD *preserves the meek in heart; From depths He rescued me.*

A deep breath puffed up Everett's chest as he tried vainly to lead
us into a rousing third stanza, urging us with his meandering arm and
flailing psalm book. It didn't work. It never did. *Serves him right,* I
thought, and belted out the last stanza particularly off-key.

O now, my soul, return again
To your own quiet rest,
Because the LORD *abundantly*
Has caused you to be blessed.
You freed from death; You dried my tears,
My stumbling feet restored.

And therefore in the land of life
I'll walk before the LORD.

As we finished, Everett's arms came down and he placed the psalter back on its shelf under the lectern, looking not just finished but defeated. He always told us that God was concerned with our hearts behind the words and not our ability to carry a tune, but he didn't believe that. You could see it frustrated him mightily to put himself through this every week. But today I cared less than usual about Everett's inflated ego. His warbling didn't make him any better than the rest of us, but on Sunday mornings it sure seemed like he thought it did.

He sat in the high-backed wooden elder's chair at the back of the raised platform, eyes cast down, as Pastor Ray moved to the microphone again. I sat through the motions of the pastoral prayer, the gathering of the tithes and offerings, two psalms, and a Scripture reading, and lulled myself into a self-reflective trance as the sermon began. Mikey stirred and got fidgety just as Ray launched into the second point of his usual four-point sermon. It was time to put Mikey in the toddlers' nursery so the people around me weren't distracted from the sermon, even if I myself wouldn't be able to listen today.

I stood out into the side aisle and reached for Mikey, who climbed into my arms and clung to me like an oversized chimpanzee. Faith looked up at me for direction.

"Come with me, hon," I said to her quietly, and she stood and put her hand in mine. "Oh, and grab my purse for me," I added, and she deftly scooped up my purse as she left the pew and joined me in the aisle. We treaded to the back of the sanctuary and headed out the back side door leading to the nursery. As I stepped into the back lobby, I looked through the window of the outside door and saw my Cobalt parked in an outer lane, easily accessible. I stopped for a moment and blinked, thinking. Then, just as quickly, I grabbed our coats off the rack in the lobby, changed course, and led Faith out the door of the church, Mikey still clinging to me.

"Mom, why are we leaving? Church isn't over, is it?" She looked back at the door, waiting for the rest of the congregation to follow us out into the parking lot. When the door remained shut, she asked me again, "Mom, why are we leaving?"

I sighed. "Faith, I just don't feel that well. I thought I could make it through the whole service, but I think I just need to get home."

She scurried up next to me as we reached the car. "You're sick all the time, aren't you?"

"I'll be fine, honey." I reached into the purse she was holding out to me and grabbed my keys to unlock the car door. I put Mikey down and opened the door, unlocking all four doors with a click and then opening the back door to allow Mikey to climb into his car seat.

While I was busy strapping belts on Mikey in the middle seat and adjusting shoulder harnesses on Faith in the booster seat just near me, I didn't hear Peter come up behind me.

"Emily, hey, there you are."

I stood up fast before backing myself out of the car and I whacked my head on the inside roof. "Ow!" I yelped, and Peter took my right arm and helped pull the rest of my upper torso out of the back seat gingerly.

"Oh, hi, Peter," I answered, rubbing the back of my head with my free hand. He let go of my arm and I turned to face him. He was blinking his innocent brown eyes at me, his sandy wavy hair bustling about in the breeze.

Faith looked up between us from her seat in the car.

"Hi, Peter!"

"Hey, Faith, I missed sitting with you this morning. How are you?"

"Fine. Mom's not fine, though. She's sick."

"Really?"

"Yeah. Again."

"Again?"

I hastily positioned myself between Peter and Faith's oversized mouth.

"Heh heh. Well, yes, I may have some sort of flu bug or something. Wasn't feeling that great after the first psalm and thought I should probably just head home and not give it to anyone else."

He frowned, pinching his eyebrows together with obvious concern. "I hadn't heard anything was going around. You okay to drive?"

Flustered and fearful he would grab my keys out of my hand and take charge, I shook my head hastily. "No, please, I'm fine, really. I just should have stayed home, that's all."

"But this isn't the first time? Sounds like you've been sick off and on."

I closed my eyes and took a quick, shallow breath before answering. "Kinda."

"That explains why you've been avoiding me."

"Avoiding you?"

"Yeah. You haven't returned my calls. Must've left half a dozen messages on your machine in the past week."

"Oh, those. Sorry about that. I've just been so scatterbrained since getting back from Easton."

"Hey, I understand. I'm just sorry you're not a hundred percent yet. I want to hear about the reunion sometime soon. I prayed for Marty like you asked me to. I hope that part went well."

My knees trembled under me and I held onto the top of the door frame. "Well, he's still not saved, if that's what you're asking me."

"Doesn't surprise me. I just wondered if he seemed receptive. I don't think I expected a pew-popping miracle or anything."

Faith started to giggle from her strapped-in spot in the back seat. "Pew-popping! Hee hee!"

"Faith," I cautioned. "Behave, please."

Peter seemed to sense my growing uneasiness. "Well, I won't keep you. You're probably anxious to get home and relax." I nodded. "If you're sure you can manage the drive ..."

I nodded harder. "Yeah, Peter, really. I just need to crash and burn a little." I stepped back and closed the back door with a solid thud. Opening my own door, I braved facing him for a moment. "I'll call you. Promise."

He laughed softly. "I've heard that before. I won't hold you to that, and I won't hold my breath, either." He raised an eyebrow at me playfully. My heart broke just a little then, and a spiral of sadness sucked me down.

"Okay," I croaked and slipped into the driver's seat, key in the ignition. After turning the engine over and putting down the window, I closed the door. Peter leaned down on the door.

"Take care, okay? You know I worry about you all alone over there in that big house."

"I know," I said, barely audible. "I'm fine."

With that, I put the car into Drive and wiggled my fingers in a silent wave as I slowly pulled out of the parking space. Peter backed up to give me room to maneuver, waving back in a heart-wrenching way that made me want to cry. I blinked the moistness from my eyes and turned the corner out of the lot, heading home.

PART TWO: GRAY

"For the guilt that binds us is our own, arising from our own sin, leaving us without the will or the capacity to do good. ... Indeed, there is no one of us with either the will or the ability to do his duty."
—John Calvin, *Institutes of the Christian Religion*

6

E VERETT NEWMAN SIPPED HOT COFFEE out of his favorite ther-
mal mug. Colombian roast, black. He put down the mug long
enough to shake the sports section open with a crisp twist of
his wrists, holding it aloft directly in front of his eyes. He hummed
Old One Hundred, the tune to Psalm 100A, one of his favorites. Up-
lifting, stalwart, strong. Admonishing the faithful to sing to the Lord
cheerfully, robustly. It was the kind of psalm that put gooseflesh on
his arms, prickly hairs on the back of his neck. Made him ache for the
coming of the Lord, sooner, not later.

Humming it didn't echo its majesty and grandeur properly, but it
brought back memories. The denominational conference, 1996. That
was the theme psalm that year, sung at every plenary session all week.
Thirteen hundred harmonizing voices lifting into the air, voices swelling, hearts swelling. Lord, it was like nothing on earth—a little piece
of heaven.

But Everett only experienced such deep joy once every four
years when the conferences were held. For the two hundred-plus
Sabbaths between conferences, Everett lumped along precenting for
the worship of Calvin Presbyterian Church, a small group of well-

meaning but poorly singing saints. It took every fiber of his being to enjoy as worship the gape-mouthed yawling that spewed toward him every Sunday morning as he beat his arms to the rhythm in his head. He tried to hear in his mind the right notes, the right harmonies, the real tune. Lord knows he rarely heard those things in real life.

Everett held on for the bimonthly presbytery-wide psalm-sings, where the Calvin yawlers were finally overpowered by the larger congregations in the presbytery, churches filled with alumni members of the Geneva College chamber choir, pastors' wives with music theory training, drama and music students from colleges as far away as Carnegie Mellon down in Pittsburgh. While precenting for his own congregation between conferences and psalm-sings, he often found himself daydreaming that he was leading a thousand-plus eager Covenanters in a theme psalm like 46C, which rang out to the tune of Martin Luther's "Ein Feste Burg." Too often, he simply turned a deaf ear to his fellow worshipers at Calvin. It was something akin to self-preservation.

On this particular morning Everett wasn't really thinking much about the congregation's singing. He was looking forward to tonight's Christian education committee meeting. It was time to finalize next year's budget for all classes, and he had heard that Emily Saunders had left yesterday's worship service early because she was ill. That meant the odds were good that she might not be in attendance tonight after all. One less naysayer would only make his job of getting the proper funding for his class that much easier. And no one would suggest postponing the entire meeting this late in the year for only one person. It felt like a sign from God.

Everett stood, folded the newspaper neatly back the way it had started, and poured a fresh cup of coffee into his Dunkin' Donuts travel mug.

"Janie!" he called, hoping his wife heard him from the back bedroom. "Gotta go, hon!" He scooped up the travel mug and then his keys as he walked past the end table near the front door. A split second before the door closed behind him, he heard a faint voice from inside call cheerily, "Bye, honey!"

He smiled.

+ + + + +

JANIE HEARD HIS MUFFLED GOODBYE as she finished combing out her graying hair.

"Bye, honey!" she called out in response, unsure if he'd heard it as the door slammed.

Her day didn't usually start this late. Usually she had time to rustle up some eggs and toast for Everett before he hurried out the door each workday morning. But this morning he'd sneaked out of bed before the alarm went off, switching it off quietly and slipping out into the living room. They'd been up late the night before, discussing the up-coming meeting and the implications if Emily Saunders wasn't there to challenge all of Everett's suggestions the way she usually did. Everett had talked animatedly, gesturing wildly about the new Reformed curriculum he wanted to see implemented in the upcoming winter classes at church. Perhaps now it would happen, with one less negative vote. Janie couldn't remember the last time she'd seen him so excited about something at Calvin.

Her husband could leap out of bed on a scant five hours' sleep and work refreshed throughout the day. He could build up a sleep deficit for days—sometimes the entire week—before having to catch up on a Saturday morning. Janie had never been so blessed. If she didn't get a full night's sleep each night, the next afternoon would turn into a blur of narcoleptic weariness and lack of productivity. Everett had appar-ently taken pity on her, since he had been the one keeping her up last night with his ongoing one-sided discussion of Christian education, and had let her sleep in.

She smiled as she stood and moved away from the dressing table, closing her robe again and slipping her feet into her bedroom slippers before scuffling out into the living room and then into the kitchen.

Yawning the last of the sleep out of her system, she moved nearer the sink across the room, catching the aroma of good coffee and grabbing a mug from the cabinet above the sink. She turned to the coffeemaker, only to find it drained of every last drop of freshly brewed coffee. She chuckled. Everett's mercy, unlike God's, extended only so far.

7

I SAID, I DON'T CARE! How many times do I have to repeat myself?"
My mouth hung open. I was astonished that it had come to
this. Everett Newman, in a classroom chair too small for his girth,
his stomach indented into the chair's attached desktop, was seething
at me from across the room. If a single button popped on his tight
oxford button-down, I was sure he'd have a stroke on the spot. I could
almost see his blood pressure going through the roof.

Granted, I'd never been Everett's favorite person, nor was he mine,
but it rarely came to such obvious verbal showdowns in the middle
of a public meeting. His wife, Janie, a dear misunderstood woman,
blanched at us both, trying to seem as if she wasn't listening at all,
wasn't hearing her husband plow over me. I almost felt sorry for her.
Almost.

The meeting had gone badly, starting right after the opening
prayer and devotions. I should have stayed home, and I sensed it from
the moment I walked into the session room a few moments after the
meeting started and saw everyone look at me with a mixture of shock
and dismay. They all assumed I was still sick. I suppose it was what I
deserved for leaving church early and fibbing about having the flu on

my way out. My stepping through the door forced them all to abandon their sense of relief that there would be no head-butting confrontation over the budget this year.

I naively assumed that Everett would take a little pity on me for what I'd gone through the month before. During an adult Sabbath school class last fall on the topic of God's mercy, he lectured us on the subtle differences in definition between mercy and pity. Pity implies a kind of condescension, a sense that the person being pitied is inherently below the one pitying. It does not necessarily imply, as mercy does, action to correct the disparate situation.

Apparently neither trait was Everett's strong suit. He had no intention of mimicking God's mercy or pity with me, only His righteousness. Or, in Everett's case, *self*-righteousness. He had blue blood in his veins, ice-cold through his heart. He gave Covenanters a bad name. And tonight was no exception.

"I said, how many times do I have to repeat myself?"

I wanted to turn tail and run, to find the doorknob again and slam the door behind me. Instead, I sat and shook visibly. Daisy Henderson leaned over and stroked my arm lightly, asking above a whisper, "Dear, are you all right?"

I nodded but shook some more. The room spun a little to the left and Everett came out of focus a bit then blurred entirely before the room spun back too far to the right, past Daisy and around to my own knees. Suddenly the world was only my knees, knocking together as I stared at them, and then I was spinning. The world was spinning.

Sitting at the end of the row, I turned and deftly reached for the metal wastepaper basket next to the small desk on my right. My head landed inside the basket just in time, amid dismayed noises and groans from the other committee members. With my fuzzy peripheral vision, I caught Everett making his way for the door.

"She should have stayed home!" he announced. "She's going to give us all the flu!"

By this time he had nearly made it to the door and was reaching for the knob. The others gasped collectively and began to gather their things hurriedly, as if I had anthrax. I was upset that Everett had painted me as someone careless enough to endanger other people.

"No!" I groaned, half into the metal basket, hearing it echo my voice more loudly than I wanted. "I'm not sick, you idiot. I'm *pregnant*."

The gasping stopped immediately. The world stopped with it. I waited desperately for their groaning to resume. Anything to break the deafening silence that now pounded in my ears.

8

JONATHAN CALVIN SAUNDERS HAD BEEN A MAN'S MAN, or at least that was the phrase most often used in our circles to describe him. I never fully knew what that meant, but I still used it sometimes. It was a handy shortcut to describe him. To me, I guess, it meant a man who had the courage to die for God, and better yet, who had the courage to *live* for God. And Jon was one of those rare men who managed to live for God most of the time. The most striking part of it all, though, was that he was never satisfied with his godly life. The years we were married I helped him carry this immense burden, trying to assure him that he was, in fact, pleasing God. He may have even suspected this, but I don't think he ever let himself really believe it, for fear that he'd slip into complacency. What an amazing energy it took to maintain such frustration with oneself! I wondered more than once if he'd have been able to live to a ripe old age and continue to hold that high level of self-dissatisfaction. If it were me, I'd have either gone crazy or given up after a while. But in God's providence, Jon didn't have to uphold his own impossible standards longer than three decades. And, also in God's providence, it seemed I would have no trouble at all living to a ripe old age.

Of course, I haven't always been so matter-of-fact about all this. It's just that I have developed this knack for being cool and witty and totally outside of an experience while I'm going through it. After it's all over, though, it sometimes sneaks back to haunt me, to delight me, or just to nag me.

After the past few years, I could now think of Jon for long periods of time without bawling at all, as long as I remained analytical and somewhat sociological in my approach. As long as I was categorizing Jon, or our relationship, or was musing philosophically about the sovereignty of God, I could sit and think about Jon all day. But the moment a certain song played on the car radio, or a particular odor filled my nose, or Mikey whined to be held like he used to do just before he learned to walk, I'd lose my tenuous grip on reality and end up in some outer limits of consciousness, with the car careening half off the road, or maybe with Mikey throwing himself onto the floor at home in a tantrum. Then reality would mercifully flood back into my body so I could deal promptly with the crisis I had just created.

And, I knew now that God was in this with me for the long haul. I was only just beginning to realize on a conscious level that God had never left me, that He had a plan for me and that I was being trained for it, day in and day out, through the petty, insignificant details of existence. And, I was going to be in training for the rest of my life.

One frightening thought crept into my mind more and more often these days. I wondered if God had taken Jonathan away from me so that I'd deal with the fact that He had a purpose for me, Emily, and not just for me, Mrs. Jonathan Saunders. In the months before Jonathan's death, I had been subconsciously measuring our spiritual maturity as one big unit, subsuming my own personal piety under Jonathan's overwhelming success in the Christian life. If he was devouring theology books fresh off the press, or getting accolades from his professors and fellow students, I figured we were both doing pretty well. It never occurred to me that, even though I could hear him read-

ing Bible stories to the kids in the den while I made down their beds
and tidied up their room before bedtime, I wasn't getting any more
spiritually mature.

✚ ✚ ✚ ✚ ✚

"Now what?" I asked.

"Uh-oh, I think I goofed."

Jonathan stared at the dead end of the hall in front of us. "Let's
turn around and go back. It's got to be here somewhere."

"It's after midnight. How come we can't find our way out of a
simple building?" I mumbled.

"It works coming from Doherty Hall to Science Hall. It just looks
different going in reverse. There must be some glitch in getting from
the fifth floor of Science to the first floor of Doherty." He was calculat-
ing this all out to himself. I walked past him and slapped him soundly
on the back.

"Nice try, Jonathan. So much for your shortcut. I have a better
idea. Let's go outside and just walk around the building like we should
have done in the first place." I motioned for him to follow me back up
the hall to find the nearest exit.

"Aw, Emily, you're no fun."

"Oh, I'm lots of fun. But, not in the middle of the night when I
have an eight-thirty class tomorrow. C'mon, please?"

"Listen, it's a matter of principle now. I'm not gonna let a stupidly
constructed building get the better of me." He stayed two paces behind me, glancing left and right again and again, trying to find the
mystery corridor that connected the newer Science Hall to the ancient
Doherty Hall. I had to keep turning around to make sure he hadn't
darted down a side hallway without me. He had the funniest little
smirk on his face, and I laughed at the sight of my master theologian
discovering that God has a sense of humor.

"What I can't figure out," Jon explained, trying desperately to ex-
onerate himself and to regain some sense of intellectual dignity in

the whole fiasco, "is how a great engineering school like CMU could construct a new building next to an old one and do such a lousy job of connecting them."

I smiled at him and nodded my head in exaggerated agreement.

"Oh, sure, go ahead, laugh," he said.

"What? I'm not laughing. Honest."

"You might as well be." He looked off to the left and saw a steel emergency exit door. "Hey, here's a way out," he said, and traipsed off down the left corridor without so much as a glance behind him to see if I was following.

"Jonathan!" I called after him. "That's an emergency exit. It'll probably set off an alarm or something if you open it."

He spun around and stopped. "Nah, it won't. Trust me."

He grinned, turned back around, and continued the rest of the way over to the door. I gave up and trotted off after him. I caught up with him in no time and patted his hip solidly. "Why I'm trusting you on this I'll never know."

"You love it," he said, and pushed on the horizontal metal bar that opened the door. It opened with little more than a loud click—no alarm, no buzzing, no wailing sirens in the night. Jonathan held the door open for me and motioned for me to go first. "See? What did I tell you?"

"All right, all right, so you were right—this time," I conceded, stepping through the door. He came through immediately after me, and the door shut behind us with a thick thud that echoed across the quad.

The crisp October night was beautifully clear. I saw the glowing white moon peek at us through the bare sycamore trees lined up neatly down the length of Baker Hall. Far off to the left, I saw three or four people in sleeping bags under two sidewalk lampposts, guarding the freshly graffitied CMU Fence against artistic intruders who might alter their message before dawn. *What a hokey ritual,* I thought fleetingly as I felt a chilling autumn breeze kick up, sail through the unprotected trees, and pick up speed across the barren quad. Few traditions were worth freezing your butt off—and this wasn't one of them.

"Pretty night," Jon said, breaking through the hushed rustling. He was right behind me, and I could feel his warm breath on the nape of my neck. I shivered, feeling gooseflesh rise on my arms and neck. I clasped my denim jacket a little closer to me.

"Yeah, it sure is," I agreed, and turned to face him. As I did, I saw just the tops of the bushes on either side of us. I looked over the metal railing that I now noticed was all around us and saw that we were two stories up, and not on the ground. Jonathan noticed it too and looked straight down at his feet. I followed his gaze down.

"Jon?"

"Uh—yes?" he answered, hesitating.

"Am I mistaken, or are we on a fire escape?"

"Um," he hedged, looking furtively on all sides of us—front, back, up and, finally, down. "I think you're right." He pointed to the long metal steps that were folded up and hanging in midair on the same parallel plane as our tiny porch. "Yeah, it's a fire escape all right."

I pushed past him and reached for the door handle that would take us back into the warmth of Science Hall—or Doherty Hall—or wherever we were. I flinched. The handle wasn't there.

"Jon?"

"Yes?" he said, and I could tell by the direction of his voice that he was still looking out at the quad.

"Why isn't there a handle on this door?"

He was beside me in a flash and was feeling around the smooth steel door where the door handle should have been. "It's gotta be here somewhere. It's just too dark to see, that's all," he explained. It sounded like he was trying to convince himself more than me.

"No, Jon, we can see just fine," I exhaled. "There are no handles on fire exit doors. Anyone who goes out isn't supposed to go back in."

There was silence, and Jon fidgeted just a little. "Oops," he finally said in a whisper. It was his way of apologizing.

"'Oops'? And how do you propose to get us out of here?" I asked, folding my arms across my chest defiantly and turning to face him.

"Well," he began, suddenly smiling and pulling me to him. I bit down on my lip to keep from smiling in return. He looked heartbreakingly handsome in the moonlight and felt delightfully warm. "I don't have any ideas. Do you?" He raised one eyebrow playfully.

"Umm, no, none."

"Well, we'll just have to stand here till we think of something."

"Gosh, Jon, with all the bright ideas you've had tonight, we could be here a while," I teased.

He instantly released me in a hands-off gesture. "Hey, if you don't like it, you can just jump down and go back to your dorm. Nobody's stopping you."

I glanced over the edge of the landing as if I were seriously contemplating his suggestion. "Nope," I decided and slipped my arms around his waist. "It's nice and warm up here." He smiled.

"I suppose we should pound on the door until one of those nerds in the computer room hears it and rescues us."

"What's your rush?" I asked, and kissed his chin lightly.

"Well, I suppose I could find a few spare minutes to stand here and neck before we scream for help," he said, rambling on as I planted little kisses on his chin and face. "I'm sure those ATO guys under the Fence won't mind."

"No, I'm sure they're used to it," I said between kisses.

He pinned me against the door and kissed me on the mouth. His lips were cold from the wind, and I felt the hair on the back of my neck stand up. It was wonderful.

He broke away slowly and gazed deep into my eyes. "This place is perfect," he whispered.

"For what?" I asked, smiling. "Besides maybe a trapeze act or something?" He was rifling through his jacket pockets as I spoke.

"For this," he said, and produced a small hinged box out of the left breast pocket of his jacket. "It's for you."

He handed it to me. The box almost fit in the palm of my hand, and I stroked the velvet covering it, staring at Jon all the while. "What is this?" I asked, trying to sound innocently curious but feeling embarrassed and a little panicky.

"Open it," he instructed simply. "I've been carrying it around for almost two weeks. It's getting a little heavy." He was grinning—and waiting.

I tore my gaze away from him and slowly looked down at the box in my hand. I caressed it, tapped it, turned it over and over, trying to put off opening it.

"What are you waiting for? Go ahead—open it."

I glanced up at him one more time for confirmation that I should go on. He nodded, still smiling. The inevitable was upon me, and I watched as my hands pried the box open painfully slowly. In the dead of the night, I heard every faint creak of the tiny hinge on the box as it resisted, as it tried to tease me by pulling itself closed again. Then, the hinge eased into a comfortable position, and the box was open. There, catching minuscule moonbeams and flashing them up to me, was a petite, simple diamond set on a delicate gold band. I turned the box slightly, and the ring winked at me.

"Oh my."

"Well?" Jon asked, unable to contain himself. "Do you like it?"

I looked at him for a moment, giving myself a little time to let everything sink in. "What does this mean?" I asked diplomatically, trying to avoid the obvious conclusion, just in case that wasn't what he had intended.

"It means, dear girl," he answered, enfolding me and the open box in his arms, "that, with your kind permission, I'd like to spend the rest of my life with you." He chastely kissed me on the cheek.

"Oh, Jon," I began, and words failed me. I looked again at the ring, and then back at Jon. "Oh, Jonathan."

He reached into the box and gently removed the ring. Before I had even thought about it, I saw my left hand thrust itself out, as if drawn to the ring like a magnet. Jon put my hand in his and slipped the ring onto my willing finger.

"Emily Weller, will you marry me?" he asked, and before I could say yes, as I felt compelled to do, he had dropped down on one knee on the cold metal gridwork of the fire escape, looking up at me expectantly and still clutching my hand.

"Oh, Jon," I sighed, still overwhelmed. I fell to my knees next to him and threw my arms around his neck.

He laughed and hugged me. "Look, I've reduced her to a two-word vocabulary! Is this a yes?"

Without letting go of him, I smiled and whispered into his ear, "Only if you get me off this fire escape before sun-up." He pulled back just far enough to look into my eyes, and then grinned. I let go of him and brushed a tear off my cheek. He stood first and put a hand down to help me up.

"Okay," he agreed, and suddenly he grabbed the metal railing and vaulted over the side of the fire escape. He clutched the railing tightly, and was now dangling over the flowerbed directly below us. He blithely hand-climbed down the three rungs of the railing and grasped the floor grid of the fire escape. With his six-foot frame and his added arm span, he was now a little more than one story above the ground. I held my breath as I watched him with giddy anxiety.

Headline: Girl engaged three minutes dies in freak fire escape mishap....

In seconds, he let go and dropped noiselessly to the dirt below, landing firmly on his feet. He held his arms up in the dismount gesture of a gymnast, and I applauded his performance.

"Bravo!"

He bowed. "Thank you! Now, you!" he shouted, and opened his arms as if I were to plummet off after him. I guffawed.

"No way, buddy. You're gonna have to come up here and open this door and get me. I'm not jumping."

"C'mon, it's not hard. I'll catch you."

"Jon, forget it."

"I thought I could talk you into just about anything."

I looked again at the ring on my left hand. "Just about anything. But not jumping off a fire escape."

He put his arms down and sighed loudly. "Okay, okay. I'll be right up," he said, and strode briskly around to the front of Doherty Hall.

In minutes, the fire door opened, and Jon beckoned me inside the building. "Doorman. Which floor, miss?"

"Hey," I said as I stepped inside the warm, quiet hallway. "How did you get up here so fast? You were dead lost before we went out-side."

He grinned wider than ever and shrugged his shoulders. "I dunno. Just lucky, I guess." He walked past me down the corridor, letting the fire door shut loudly behind me. He looked back over his shoulder at me and winked.

"Why, you little sneak!" I called and dashed after him. He heard my quick footfalls and broke into a run, laughing wildly.

"Catch me if you can!"

I picked up my pace in a vain attempt to close the ever-widening gap between us. He turned the corner and never slowed, still howling with laughter. The echo of it rang in my ears, and I stopped at the corner, letting myself sink onto the floor, trying to catch my breath through my uncontrollable giggling.

He stopped dead, turned, and called back to me. "Ya know, Em, someday you're gonna look back on all this and laugh."

+ + + + +

JONATHAN TOOK COMMAND, as was his custom in potentially awk-ward or embarrassing situations like this. "Let me handle it," he said, and I sidled in just behind his shoulder. The man at the counter glared at us, looking impatient. "We have a reservation for Mr. and Mrs. Jonathan Saunders." I instinctively blushed. The man ran his finger down the open page of the day's reservations and stopped at our names.

"Yes, here it is, sir. Three nights. Will that be cash or charge?"

"Cash, please," Jon said quickly, and reached into his back pocket to take out his wallet. He fumbled for a moment, and I took pity on him and picked it out of his pocket for him.

He paid the man for all three nights, and the man gave him a scribbled receipt. We both turned away from the desk, grateful for a change of scenery from the man's sour puss.

"Sir?"

"Yes?" Jon responded, turning back around.

"Your key, sir," he said flatly, dangling the room key in front of him.

Jon put down the heavy suitcases he had just picked up and snatched the key out of the man's hand. "Thanks," he said tersely, and picked the suitcases back up again. We walked to the elevator, and I pressed the up button.

"What a pleasant fellow," Jon said sarcastically.

"He needs a little more fiber in his diet," I agreed. "Jon, can I help you with just one of those?"

"Oh, that's a laugh," he said. "Like you could carry one of these things when it's empty, let alone stuffed to the gills."

"Okay, so I'm not muscle-bound like you. So what?"

"I'm not complaining," he clarified, and grinned at me. I blushed again. This kind of innocent innuendo had been funny for the past year, but now it was obviously put-up or shut-up. I had never been so nervous, and especially about something that most of my friends were already taking for granted. I must have been the only virgin left in the entire crowd, both from high school and college. That is, except probably for Marty. And now, of course, Jonathan too. I grinned back at him, this time without blushing. *God's in His heaven, and all's right with the world*, I thought.

The elevator door opened and we went up to the fifth floor. Our room was at the far end of the hall, and I took the lead, glancing at the numbers on the doors as we passed.

"Wait, master," Jonathan said from behind me. I turned and saw him pretending to be weighed down with the baggage, dragging the suitcases along the velvety carpet and shuffling along in an exaggerated, lopsided gait.

I laughed. "Oh, now you look like me, for cryin' out loud."

He straightened and walked normally the rest of the way to the room. "Wouldn't that be embarrassing?" he joked.

I slipped the key out from between the suitcase handle and the palm of his hand, and opened the door to our room. He stepped in past me and flopped the suitcases onto the bed. "Uh-oh," he said, as he glanced around the room.

"What?" I asked, worried that something major had gone wrong already.

"There's only one bed. Where are you gonna sleep?" He grinned again.

At least he's got a sense of humor about all this. But, then again, he can afford to—he's the man.

"I'll sleep on the floor."

"Really? I pictured you as more conventional than that, Em. I've always heard something about the 'missionary position.' That sounds pious."

I balked. "Jonathan!" I was taken aback by his off-color comments. "Do all men do this? Is this some kind of defense mechanism or something?" I asked.

"Oh, go ahead, treat me like an object." He sat down on the bed between the suitcases and covered his face with his hands. "No, I'm serious: treat me like an object." I laughed nervously. "You just want me for my mind," he sniffled, and peeked out through his fingers to see if I was going to play along.

"Now, Jonathan," I began, walking toward him and working up the courage to sit on his lap—something I had done dozens of times before without consequence. "That's not true. I don't want you just for your mind." I smiled. He uncovered his face completely and put his arms around me. "I want you for your adjusted gross income potential, too," I quipped.

"I'm gonna pretend I didn't hear that. And now," he added, "I can't wait to get started on married life. How about you?"

The pretense of innuendo was being stripped away rapidly, and I was beginning to feel light-headed. "What do you mean?" I asked, determined to make him work for everything.

"I mean," he started, and stood up, forcing me to get my feet back onto the floor so I wouldn't fall, "let's act like we're married, and do what all our married friends at church do."

"Oh," I said, still a little amazed that he was being so straightforward. He had never been shy about his eager anticipation of this moment, but I honestly hadn't pictured him talking us through it. "Like what?"

"Like this!" he exclaimed, and opened the drawer of the little nightstand next to the bed. He took out the old Gideon Bible that was in it and held it up for me to see. "Let's have family worship!" he said sweetly, and I fell onto the bed in laughter. He dropped the Bible onto the nightstand, and pushed both suitcases off the bed. They hit the floor with a muffled double-thump. He climbed onto the bed and hovered over me on all fours, still grinning.

"I was just kidding," he said, leaning down and kissing me for the first time since we had gotten into the car after the reception. My heart was pounding in my throat, and I felt as if I might have fainted, but I couldn't have stopped him if I wanted to. And, best of all, I didn't want to.

9

I WAS LIFELESS ON THE COUCH WHEN THE DOORBELL RANG. Faith and Mikey were playing some Super Mario Nintendo thing in the other room, and I was trying to relax by listening to their innocent chatter about things they find infinitely more important than Mommy not feeling well again. Although I was not really in the mood to see anyone, I knew it wasn't a good idea to hide forever. The more I laid around feeling sorry for myself, not answering the doorbell and letting the machine get my phone calls, the harder it would be to resurface. And eventually I would have to resurface.

Finding resolve where I thought I had none, I climbed off the couch, standing too fast and feeling my head spin a little. The ten paces to the door were difficult but well worth the effort once I opened the door and saw Meg standing there with a Pyrex dish in her hands. Empathy oozed from her pores today like sweat from mine in August. I sighed and my shoulders sagged in relief.

"Oh, thank God it's only you. Come on in."

"Emily, as soon as I heard I threw together a casserole for ya for lunch and had to bring it right on over." Meg continued to chatter as she flitted past me and headed straight for the kitchen. I closed the front door quietly and turned to follow her. She scurried into the kitchen, her unscuffed white walking shoes making squeaky noises on the linoleum floor as she rounded past the table toward the counter-top nearest the stove.

"I just knew you wouldn't want to be cooking at a time like this, and I was already making the same casserole for Sherry and Joe and the new baby, so making one more really didn't seem like a bother or anything."

She carefully set the dish down on the counter and fussed with the foil covering it.

"It's not too spicy or strong. Just a chicken and rice thing, some-thing to fill you up and get you through for another day. Do your kids like rice?"

"They do now."

"Because if they don't, you could always throw a few tater tots on a cookie sheet real quick for them, to go with the chicken. Nothing weird on the chicken. It's just all baked together in a cream of chicken soup mixture. They should be fine with it."

"Thanks, Meg. This is definitely a lifesaver today." Joining her at the counter, I lifted up the casserole and turned toward the refrigera-tor.

"Listen, Meg, I don't know what you heard, or how you might have heard it, but—"

Apparently sensing the impending awkwardness, she interrupted me. "Emily, get those bad thoughts out of your head right now."

"What bad thoughts?"

"No one thinks badly of you or anything. No one thinks you brought any of this on yourself. Everyone seems real supportive. Are you going to contact the police?"

The police?

"It hadn't really occurred to me. Why?"

"I mean the Easton police. You know, and let them know you know more about what happened to you when you were attacked."

I stared at her blankly, unable to put two and two together.

"You know ..." She leaned in to me and whispered. ". . . Now that you know you must have been *raped* and all."

The muscles in my hands and arms went numb, sending the glass casserole dish—and the chicken and rice—smashing to the kitchen floor in a gooey shattered mess no newly pregnant woman would want to clean up. Meg and I both stared at the glop and glass covering the floor for what seemed an interminable amount of time.

"Oh, Emily, I'm sorry. I shouldn't have said the 'r' word. Here, let me get that taken care of." She bent down and began picking up the largest of the glass pieces with her bare hands.

"Meg, stop that! I'll get it. This was my fault. I'm a klutz. I'm so sorry about your dish." I stooped down next to her, plucking smaller shards from the rice and soup ooze that had puddled out across the floor.

Meg stood. "Where's your dust pan and some paper towels?" she asked authoritatively, sauntering to the trash can in the corner and delicately placing the glass pieces inside the bag. "We can get this up in a jiffy before the kids come out here and step in the glass."

Without really considering the bad etiquette in letting a friend clean up my kitchen floor for me, I answered, "In the entryway to the basement over there," pointing with one hand while nabbing still smaller pieces of glass with my other hand. I stood and walked to the can myself, adding my collection of broken glass to the pile.

Proper tools in hand, Meg efficiently swiped up the glop of chicken and rice with the paper towels and dust pan, carrying it neatly to the trash can and making sure it was all safely inside. She went to the sink to wash off the dust pan, still running on all cylinders, as usual.

"Emily, now listen, I think for dinner tonight we should maybe just order a pizza. What do you say? Want some company?" She smiled so sweetly that I nearly blushed at the genuineness of it.

"Actually, that sounds pretty good right now." Pizza sounded great, but more than that—so did the prospect of hearing what all the buzz was around the congregation in the hours since I dropped my little bombshell during the Christian education meeting last night. Apparently Meg had already heard quite a bit, enough to form some fairly solid opinions. I was curious to hear these opinions traced back to their original sources. It would also be interesting to see which part of me won out tonight, the gossip-sleuth or the attack victim with fuzzy memories. I wondered how big a role Everett Newman played in the dissemination of vital information. Me, always the skeptic, at least about Everett. But he—of all people—deserved my skepticism. I had rarely been wrong about the man in the past ten years.

Meg was at the phone near the fridge and plucked it off its cradle, apparently dialing Pizza Joe's, a number everyone within a ten-mile radius knew by heart, even the ever-together Meg. It looked strange to see Meg ordering pizza. Didn't quite seem her style in some odd way. But, if I looked at it from the perspective of efficiency and appropriateness, then Meg playing dial-a-pizza made a ton of sense. Meg was nothing if not the epitome of efficiency and appropriateness. For once that part of her didn't intimidate me, and I welcomed the take-charge role. As usual, I felt a bit queasy and I wasn't up to problem-solving minute dilemmas like casserole dishes on the floor and dinner in the trash with bits of glass embedded in it. A stuffed-crust pizza with extra cheese healeth all wounds.

+ + + + +

CONVERSATION AROUND THE FLAT CORRUGATED BOX emblazoned with "Made Hot and Fresh Just For YOU!" wasn't very illuminating. Faith and Mikey, although they liked chicken, were ecstatic to over-hear Meg ordering pizza for everyone and assumed there was some special occasion they weren't aware of.

"No, dears," Meg corrected, "it's no big deal. I'm just visiting your mom and had to figure out a new dinner idea once we dropped the chicken." I knew the kids wouldn't associate the chicken and rice with a special occasion, so this truthful explanation made perfect sense to their one-track minds.

Faith's brow furrowed as Meg spoke, while Mikey sat cross-legged in front of the television, a short plastic Barney tray table over his legs, chowing down on a chewy crust I insisted he finish before starting a second slice he would probably not even finish.

"Mom, will I get glass all in my feet if I walk around in the kitchen?"

"No, Faith, I think we got it all up. Why?"

"I wanna get more juice."

"Sure, that's fine. It's in the fridge behind the iced tea. Just be careful you don't spill it."

She stood up quickly, laughing as she went. "That's funny. My *mom* telling *me* not to spill anything."

I glanced at Meg and saw her hiding a laugh behind her hand, which was cupped over her mouth. Faith caught this as she went past Meg and the two of them stifled their combined hilarity quite well, considering. Faith shook her head and continued into the kitchen, making a beeline for the refrigerator. I couldn't understand how she could drink orange juice with pepperoni pizza, even if I myself had a penchant for milk with potato chips.

As soon as Faith was outside of earshot Meg lowered her hand and the smile disappeared from her face. She looked toward me furtively, then leaned in close to speak without Mikey hearing us.

"What are you going to do now?"

I blinked, trying not to look as if I was caught off-guard by this otherwise obvious question. For all anyone around here knew, I had been raped that night during the attack over a month ago. After all, how else would a godly, single Christian woman get pregnant? I longed for the world Meg lived in, a world where people never got inappropriately pregnant, where life events followed their proper timeline, and where only Inherently Evil Persons such as Hitler, Stalin, Hussein—and possibly Everett Newman on a bad day—could botch things up really badly.

I didn't live in that world. I didn't even live in the same area code as that world. I had never even *heard* of that world until joining Calvin Presbyterian Church ten years ago. That world evoked a sense of poignant melancholy, being around this extended family—me, a lowly sinner capable of just about anything, right under their noses. It felt incredibly dishonest, as if I had betrayed each of them personally, one at a time.

The churning in my stomach throughout dinner wasn't from the pepperoni. While trying to finish at least one slice of pizza to keep my strength up and listening to Meg chat innocently with the kids, I had time to roll over in my head the possibility that I hadn't been merely beaten up last month. Hardly seemed possible, but I still didn't remember much more about the attack, which meant all bets were off, didn't it? Still, I knew better.

"Emily? You okay?"

I swung my mind back to Meg on the couch and flashed a wan smile.

"Yeah, fine. Just wish I could remember what really happened that night." *Liar!* I had no desire whatsoever to remember any more than I already knew, which was too much. This new complication, this pregnancy, this *baby* (I might as well start getting used to that concept now) would change all that. I might have to force myself to remember more. God only knew how I was going to accomplish that feat because I envisioned myself a wholly unwilling hypnosis patient.

Meg pinched her eyebrows together. "No, Emily, you don't want to remember any more of that terrible night. You've suffered enough anguish. Don't even try."

My puzzled expression must have been plain.

"Why put yourself through that? Now you know what happened, right? It must've happened while you were unconscious, praise God. Better not to have any of that to dredge up along with everything else you've been through."

She shook her head forcefully, taking a motherly tone with me that I might have found endearing and soothing had the situation been different.

"You're absolutely right." *In different circumstances, maybe.* "There's nothing to be done about it now except to move on." *Toward what, exactly?* "I have to talk to Peter about what all this means." *Oh, and Marty.*

Meg sat upright and started to reply in a shocked, loud voice but quickly brought it down to a faint whisper as she saw Faith making her way back to the living room with a cup of juice.

"You mean you haven't ... talked to Peter yet?"

I shook my head subtly and we turned our attention back to the kids. She shook her head in return. Apparently that wasn't the right answer.

Talking to Peter. Talking to Marty. Talking to God. There were too many guys to talk to, and not enough emotional reserves. The rest of the pizza in the box was clearly going to be tomorrow's breakfast because I wasn't very hungry. Again. This dilemma was quickly turning into a weight-loss program of mammoth proportions. But obviously even that side benefit couldn't last too much longer.

+ + + + +

FLIMSY PAPER PLATES AND USED PAPER NAPKINS embossed with fruits and vegetables were tossed into the trash can on top of the chicken glop and broken glass. Meg stayed to help me commandeer the kids upstairs into their bedroom on the pretense of getting into their jammies and brushing their teeth. She deftly put Faith in charge of Mikey, commissioning her as a Big Girl Now, which Faith took very seriously. Wee thing that she was herself, Faith yet managed to get Mikey to march upstairs to her rhythm, instinctively making the carpeted steps a mountain-climbing adventure for him to conquer. I stood in awe of her innate ability to take leadership. If I hadn't know better, I'd have sworn she was Meg's daughter and not mine. *Oh good, that's just what I'd need: another kid of questionable parentage.*

Meg waited until she heard Faith and Mikey's voices fade out of range before sidling up next to me at the kitchen sink.

"I'm surprised Peter hasn't called you yet today."

I tried hard to sound nonchalant. "Why? We don't really talk to each other *every* day."

She spluttered. "B-but, today. I mean, *today* ..."

"What about today?" I asked bluntly, swirling a knife around in the steamy soapy water.

She nudged at my shoulder with her own. "Emily, you know."

Yes, I knew. And she knew I knew. And I knew *she* knew I knew. And so on and so on, *ad infinitum*.

"Meg, by now he's probably in a shock-induced coma, hooked up to a ventilator over at West Side General. Remind me to pick him up a nice bouquet of miniature carnations." Hot water splashed around my fingers pleasantly.

"I don't know what to make of that," she said flatly. Meg rarely appreciated my sarcasm. She thought it wasn't very Christian. Maybe she was right.

"Or does he like daisies? I can never remember." *Swish swish.* Another knife was now squeaky clean and in the dish drainer.

"Emily, come on. One of you has to make the first move. Might as well be you."

"Then again, if he's in a coma, he won't even know whether I brought carnations or daisies. Maybe I'll just pick up whatever's cheapest." *Swoosh. Gurgle.* My water glass rinsed off easily and stood inverted in the drainer next to my coffee mug from this morning.

"Emily! He's probably in as much shock and pain over this as you are."

"Oh, I sincerely doubt that." I fished for the last fork trolling around the bottom of the sink, avoiding my grasp, as Meg moved across the room, eyeing me from a slight distance. I found the wayward fork and turned from Meg momentarily to scrub it hard in frustration.

Meg walked behind me and grabbed the phone off its cradle on the wall. She handed the receiver out to me. "Are you going to call him, or should I?"

I turned to her, hands soapy and dripping. "Why? Do you have something to tell him too?"

"Emily! It's not like he hasn't heard by now."

"So why call him then?" I protested, petulant.

"Because he should have heard it from you, not Daisy or Everett or Lord knows who else." She held the handset out more forcefully, a little closer.

"I know you're right, but I can't call him. Not yet. I need some time to think."

She softened, her shoulders sagging a little. Returning the phone to its cradle, she came close to me. "I'm so sorry, Em," she said softly. "I can't imagine what you must be going through."

"You have no idea."

She hugged me and I nearly broke. Instead I sighed. She hugged me tighter.

"Will you be okay here the rest of today alone with the kids?"

"Yeah, I'll be fine. In fact, a day alone might be just what I need to clear my head, y'know?"

"I know exactly what you mean." She scooped up her purse from the side counter and walked past the trash can. "Do you want me to take the trash out for you on my way out?"

"No, it'll be fine till tomorrow right where it is. Thanks, though. You've been a lifesaver today. It would have been bad not to see *anybody* all day."

"You're absolutely right," she agreed, heading for the back door. "Call me tomorrow morning to let me know you're all right, okay?"

I nodded, smiling. The back door snapped closed behind her, and I was alone in the kitchen. I stared at the phone on the wall for a few precious moments, unsure whether to tear it out of the jack or ignore it and watch TV instead. Five minutes stretched toward ten as I methodically scrubbed down every inch of the countertop, the phone catching my eye every time I turned in that direction. When the pots were sparkling spotlessly and the sink was scoured within an inch of its life, I couldn't stand it anymore and strode to the phone.

My trembling hands found the small address book dangling from a bulletin board next to the phone and my fingers thumbed the pages. Soon I was dialing the number, wanting to take back each press of my finger, to undo the impending connection.

But I couldn't find anything to induce that inertia, and the numbers punched one after another. Then there was a light click and the phone rang, my madly pounding heart making my ears work harder to hear it. Once. Twice. Three times. *Ring ring ring.*

Just as I was about to hang up in relief, able to say I'd tried my best, there was a louder click and a familiar voice at the other end.

"Hello?"

I had so many things to say but couldn't think of a single one.

"Hi ... it's me."

"Emily? Emily, is that you?"

I cleared my throat, hoping to hear my own voice over the hammering in my chest.

"Yeah, Marty, it's me."

10

ARTY EMERSON WASN'T A BEAUTIFUL MAN. And he hadn't been a particularly good-looking teenager. As a child he had often been overlooked due to his rather common looks: watery gray eyes, slight ectomorphic build, unstable voice that cracked at the worst possible moments. As far back as he could remember, Marty had gained admiring smiles from only a few people, mostly just his mother and Emily Weller ... that is, Emily Weller *Saunders*.

Today, as on most days, Marty left his job working as a shift manager at Wal-Mart and headed farther away from home rather than toward it. The YMCA ten miles beyond the Wal-Mart was well worth the trip, at least psychologically. He pulled into his usual spot in the parking lot, backing in his rattling green Plymouth Valiant, and grabbed his duffel bag from the passenger seat.

Marty jumped out of the car, forgetting to lock the door, and was twenty feet away before he realized it, in a hurry to get in the building and out of the developing drizzle. He stopped short, turned back to look at the unlocked car, and debated leaving it unlocked rather than going back. Had he left anything of value in plain sight in the car? Half-finished plastic bottle of Diet Mountain Dew, nearly empty pack of sugar-free gum, some old cassettes of his favorite jazz artists. Nothing anyone would want to steal in the hour or so he'd be inside the gym. He turned back toward the front door of the gym and didn't give it another thought. The gum was going to have to fend for itself.

Inside the warm dryness of the gym, Marty shed his coat and slung it over his arm. He passed the muscle-bound men whose lives revolved around the Nautilus machines and headed for the treadmills. In his haste, he bumped into a woman coming out of an aisle between two rows of stationary bikes.

"Oh, excuse me," he said instinctively, turning to smile at her. Smiling back at him was a small freckled brunette with straight hair that cupped her face under her chin. Her nose crinkled up when she smiled back at him.

"My fault," she offered, blinking sweetly up at him. He held his smile. She blushed and turned away, focusing her attention back on the stationary bike she'd been heading toward when Marty bumped into her.

Marty tore his gaze away from her and continued toward the treadmills across the open space of the main room of the gym. He was still smiling as he came to an open treadmill and dropped his duffel at the front of the machine. He didn't notice that the brunette was still eyeing him periodically. She apparently thought she inspired his smiles, and she took pleasure in seeing him grinning off into space as he jogged on the treadmill.

Only Marty knew what was making him smile. Reminders of Emily. Perky, petite, brunette. All Emily. Always Emily. Even the freckles were the same. Since their class reunion last month, he saw Emily everywhere. Except for a small card and an e-mail after she was attacked, he hadn't heard from her since the reunion, but he knew she thought of him often. He'd known her since seventh grade—her thought patterns, foibles, and frets. She didn't easily forget people, and last month had proved that.

His feet pounded the treadmill rhythmically. Left. Down. Right. Down. Faster. Faster. Harder.

That damned reunion, though. Self-forgiveness hadn't come easily. Although Emily didn't blame him for the attack, he knew it wouldn't have happened if things had gone differently right after the reunion. If she hadn't needed to take that head-clearing walk.

Wishful thinking. He couldn't change things now. The best he could do was make amends as needed and be there for Emily if she needed him. Still, memories of that ill-fated night dogged him. He couldn't run fast enough on the treadmill to get away from them. Left. Right. Down. Down.

No, it wasn't working.

As he kept trying to pound away the memories, the cell phone in the pocket of his zippered sweatshirt rang.

"Emily? Emily, is that you?"

+ + + + +

THE DISC JOCKEY HAD PUT ON "STAND BY ME," by Ben E. King, and flocks of people stood and migrated to the dance floor like so many geese in formation. Marty waved at Emily, raised an eyebrow, and pointed to the steady stream of couples weaving past them around the tables. He leaned over the table, and Emily met him halfway.

"Ya wanna?" The last slow dance of the reunion. It was so cliché. Worse than being in high school, really.

"Yeah." She shot up quickly, making it to her feet even before Marty did. He stood, straightened his tie and jacket, trying to look gentlemanly, and offered her his hand. He saw her blush unexpectedly. They raised their clasped hands over Hank's head and met on the other side.

Hank rolled his eyes at them. "Oh, will you get a load of this shit?"

Emily blushed again.

"Grow up!" Marty countered playfully, sticking out his tongue and mugging exaggeratedly for Hank. Jill and Hannah broke out laughing, and Todd grinned. As Marty and Emily left the microcosm of their table, he swore he saw Hannah nudge Jill in the side and wink.

Marty held tightly onto her fingertips as he led her around the candlelit tables of classmates to the dance floor. Familiar faces smiled up at them graciously as they squeezed past, and Marty felt a surge of emotion whip through him as he smiled back at each adult face. It hardly seemed possible that none of them looked eighteen anymore. More than once he had the feeling that they weren't really in their thirties, that they were a bunch of teenagers pretending they were all grown up and leading meaningful, responsible, important lives. They passed a table full of acquaintances from his senior gym class who were passing around photos of their children, exchanging anecdotes, and chattering away happily. Were these the same guys who, like him, week after week hastily showered after forty minutes of touch football and dressed hurriedly, eyes cast down, relieved to finally have those boxers on and to feel those jeans button closed? Were they really sitting there trading child-rearing stories? Was this possible? And, why did he feel this fleeting urge to pull up a chair and join them? He'd never fit in—not then, and not now.

Emily's light squeeze of his hand led him out of his musing. As he continued past, he looked away from their table and up at her. She looked as if she'd guessed his thoughts because she smiled sweetly at them and motioned to him gently with her head toward the dance floor. Marty hadn't lost his adolescent admiration and awe for the feminine, maternal side of women. It had always shaped his relationships with members of the opposite sex. Besides his ever-demure mother and his older sister, Emily had been the only other recipient of Marty's chivalrous behavior. And tonight he planned to shower her in that attention once again.

They reached the dance floor and squeezed their way past the tight bunches of couples into a sparser section. Marty turned, still holding Emily's hand, and extended his other arm for her. She took his other hand, and he pulled her close. They had danced together once or twice before, at school dances and chorus parties, and he'd always liked the way they fit. Marty's flair for gentlemanly behavior had some of its finest moments in circumstances like this. He almost glowed with it, and this night was no exception. He stood taller, straighter, happy to be together like this again.

As they danced slowly among the other couples, Marty felt a kind of cleansing inside, the closing of an old wound that had never quite healed properly before now. They had survived adolescence, the distance of college, and outrageous differences in theology. Their friendship and loyalty had survived through it all.

Emily moved a wee bit closer to Marty, and he beamed. Life rarely got better than this.

The other couples were all conversing as they danced, but he and Emily had moved beyond that stage of communication. They had exhausted every topic under the sun while back in Easton together the last two days, and now they had time to just be next to each other. Emily timidly laid her head on his shoulder, and he put both his arms around her. She sighed.

"You having fun?" he asked.

She tipped her head up to look at him. "Yeah. Just like old times, huh?"

He smiled. "Better."

"Yeah, better. Why is that?"

"I have no idea. You're still an uppity Calvinist. But for some reason, it doesn't bother me as much as it used to."

"Well," she said, returning her head to its comfortable place on his shoulder, "if it's any consolation, it still bothers the bejeebies out of me that you're not."

He threw back his head and laughed. "See? In high school that would have sent me over the edge."

"But not now?"

"No, not now."

Emily closed her eyes and smiled. "Then I must be slipping. Did I mention lately that you're going to hell?" she asked, exaggeratedly batting her eyelashes.

He chuckled. "No, but I figured I still was."

"Okay. Just wanted to remind you."

"Thanks."

"Don't mention it."

They were silent for a while, dancing to the second half of "Stand By Me." Emily put her arms around Marty's collar and sniffled into his neck. He pulled his head back to look down at her. "Emily, you getting sentimental on me?"

"I love you" was all she managed to squeak out without breaking into sobs.

He was both happy and confused to hear this. "I love you too, Em. Did I miss something?"

"Never mind." Emily seemed a bit more composed, her head still nestled up around his shoulder.

"It's not every day a sexy dame like you tells me she loves me. What did I do right?" he asked, trying to keep the conversation from taking on an embarrassingly emotional tone in the middle of the dance floor.

Emily sniffled again and laughed. "It's not that. I just worry about you, you know?"

Marty nodded in understanding. "Oh, that. Don't worry so much. You'll give yourself an ulcer." He kissed her on the forehead.

"I'm afraid I don't worry about you enough." She let go of his neck and put her arms around his waist instead.

The song ended and the next one was a bit too loud for both of them. Marty reached behind his back and took hold of her hands, bringing them around front.

"Do you wanna go back to the table, or go outside and talk?"

"I'm not sure. I don't have my fire-and-brimstone speech prepared," she admitted.

He smiled. "What would I do without my second mommy to keep an eye on me?"

"All right, all right," she added, letting go of one of his hands to swipe a tear off her cheek. "Go ahead, make fun of me. You know you wouldn't have it any other way."

"I suppose not," he agreed, and held her face in his hands, tilting her head up to look at him. "I really don't know what I'd do without you," he said, low and hoarse.

Hannah appeared out of nowhere, suddenly tapping Marty on the shoulder. Marty instantly let go of Emily's face.

"A-*hem*," she interrupted slyly. "You guys about ready to ditch this dump? I could use that ride back to my parents' place now."

Emily looked over at her. Hannah already had her coat on and her purse slung over her shoulder and was carrying all the papers, programs, and notes they had been saddled with that night. She also had Emily's coat, purse, and yearbook, and held them aloft for Emily to take from her.

Emily took them and blinked up at Marty. "I guess it's about time to leave, huh?"

Marty shrugged. "Yeah, let's split. But, let's say goodbye to everybody first."

After they'd made the rounds, they found Hannah again at the main doorway of the ballroom. Marty pushed open the door for Hannah and Emily, and Hannah stepped through first. He followed them, and they walked together in silence out the front door and toward Marty's Valiant, hearing the music growing fainter as they walked. By the time they reached the car, all Marty heard were the scuffling, syncopated rhythms of their footfalls on the blacktop. He unlocked the passenger door and Hannah slid in first, becoming an effective barrier between him and Emily. He plopped into the driver's seat and tried to get the Valiant to turn over. It gave in and started on the third long try, and the rattly purr of the engine and the tinny voices coming from the AM radio were all they shared on the seemingly endless trip from Allentown to Easton.

✝ ✝ ✝ ✝ ✝

HANNAH GOT OUT OF THE CAR AND SHUT THE DOOR. Emily rolled down the passenger window and Hannah leaned inside just a little.

"Well, it's been real."

"Hey," Emily said, "we didn't get that group picture like we said we would."

"Oh, damn."

"I know," Marty suggested, "we'll all just have to go out for breakfast tomorrow."

Hannah rolled her eyes. Emily laughed.

"No, I'm serious. We'll all still be here, right? We should do it. It'll be fun. Besides, we haven't raided Hank's parents' house all at the same time for years. We'll have to stop over there. I wonder if they still have that antique spittoon in the rec room."

"Oh no," moaned Hannah, "the old fake-spit-and-clink-the-bottom trick!"

Marty flushed and grinned, trying to look as if such a stunt was beneath him at his age.

Hannah thumped the side of the car with her fist. "You never change, do you? You'll be an asshole till the day you die, Marty Emerson." She winked. "Well, guys, I'm not used to being out this late. Must be getting old." She winked again.

"I'm not used to it, either," Emily agreed. "Usually I'm in the house after the kids' bedtime. I think I'm running on adrenaline."

Hannah straightened and backed away from the car slowly, talking as she went. "Whatever you decide about tomorrow, call me before eleven. After that I'll probably be out most of the afternoon. I can help call a few people if you want."

"Great," Marty called after her. "We just might take you up on that. I'll call you around nine-thirty or ten."

"Okay. Be good!" She turned, waved slightly, and walked methodically up to the porch. She climbed the steps, opened the door, disappeared inside, and switched off the porch light without looking back at us. Marty and Emily were plunged into total darkness. The streetlights started nearly two blocks up, closer to the main intersection.

Marty started the car and backed out of the driveway, throwing his right arm over the back of the seat to look behind him as he backed out. "Whaddya think? A trip to Norris Fun Park tomorrow'd be wild, wouldn't it?"

"Norris Fun Park? Don't you remember the last time we were all there? The night before you left for college?"

"I remember," Marty said in an eerily soft voice.

"The place was deserted."

A strange, uncomfortable silence fell over them. Marty put the car in drive and started toward the lone stop light at the end of Hannah's street. "I know," he admitted, "but at least we were all together."

She sighed. "But we were miserable." Sadness and melancholy had created a special, bittersweet bond all their own. It was as though their group bond of loyalty tightened its hold on them all that last night—in a grip so tight they couldn't help bursting and flying off in different directions.

Marty shook his head and *tsk-tsked* at her.

"What a maroon," he said, in his passable Bugs Bunny voice.

"Just keep driving—and watch where you're going."

He grinned. "Yes, dear."

+ + + + +

MARTY YANKED HIS KEYS OUT OF THE IGNITION and got out of the car, slamming the door as usual. Without thinking, Emily gathered up her purse and papers and opened the passenger door. She swung her legs daintily out of the car and planted her pumps firmly down, heels digging inadvertently into Marty's toes. He had come around to her side of the car to help her out, and she had promptly stepped on his feet.

"Ouch." He smiled.

"You seem to say that a lot. Sorry." She pulled her feet up and put them back down on either side of his.

"Here, let me help you." He reached out a hand. She shifted her papers and purse into one arm and took Marty's hand with her free hand. He pulled her straight up, and they were suddenly standing face to face in the quiet parking lot.

"It seems we've raised the stakes a lot since we were kids," he said softly.

They walked all the way to the door of Emily's room in relative silence, her toying with her keys and Marty whistling airily beside her. She opened the door and beckoned him inside. He followed, brushed past her, and turned on the television as she dropped her things onto the dresser. He stood watching the television as he took off his jacket, draping it over the desk chair after extracting his keys out of the pocket and tossing them onto the dresser.

"Turn the channel," Emily begged when she saw the World Wrestling Entertainment logo flash onto the screen. Marty laughed.

"Okay, okay." He flipped past some football game highlights and stopped at a channel with a commercial, waiting to see what would follow.

Emily got off the other bed where she was sitting and walked around the corner into the tiny bathroom, leaving the door slightly ajar.

"That feels so much better," was all he heard from the bathroom.

"Emily, that's gross."

She stepped out of the bathroom, holding a pair of stretched-out pantyhose in front of her. "I was just taking these things off."

"Oh, I thought you were peeing," he said bluntly and grinned, then turned his attention to the TV, which was bringing them back into the middle of an old Joan Crawford movie. "Do you want to watch this?" he asked over his shoulder, in a tone that translated, "You don't, do you?"

"Nah, just find something tolerable for background noise." She plopped back down on the first bed.

"Okay," he said and began his channel-clicking ritual all over again. *Click. Click. Click-click-click.*

"Marty! Just stop at the first inoffensive thing and sit down, will you?"

"All right." He stopped at what looked like some old PBS special on fungus. "Lord love a duck, this should liven up the conversation a bit." He sat down on the other bed, then fell backwards and lay sprawled across the bedspread, sighing loudly. "What a night!"

"You know, though, I don't think I could handle this more than once every five years."

"Did you see the way everybody at the table looked at us when we got up to dance?" he said, changing the topic.

"I noticed that, but I thought I was just feeling paranoid about it—like they were all waiting for it or something."

"I think they were taking bets on us, and when that last dance hit, everybody cashed in their chips."

"Hank was the only one who looked peeved," Emily observed.

"Well, there isn't much these days that doesn't piss him off," Marty admitted. "We were just the subject at hand at that moment."

"I wish there was something we could do for him." Emily seemed to slump into a melancholy state, apparently remembering the perpetually dismal look plastered on Hank's face all night.

"You can pray for him. You like to do that sort of thing." He wasn't teasing her this time.

"I know, but I'd like to be able to actually *do* something."

"And you call yourself a Calvinist," Marty said coyly and turned over to look at her and smiled.

"Oh, c'mon, you know what I mean." She smiled herself. "Cut it out. Haven't you had enough for one weekend?"

"Em, do you ever think we'll get past this?"

"Get past what?"

"Past theology? Past doctrine? Past God?"

"Nope," she said simply. "Not unless those scales fall off your eyes someday. There's a Bible in the nightstand here if you want to borrow it."

Marty turned back over and groaned. "You're hopeless."

Getting up from the far bed, she walked over to her suitcase and flipped it open. "Where are my PJ's?"

"Are you ever-so-subtly kicking me out?" Marty asked, having heard her and sitting upright on the other bed.

"What?" She turned around to see him waiting for her to answer. "Oh, no. Don't be silly. I just wanted to get out of this annoying dress. I hate dressing up."

"Pity. You looked so nice tonight. You should do it more often."

"Nice? Really?"

"You were a knockout ... as usual." He grinned openly, and she blushed. It was a wholly subjective opinion—one that might not have been shared by many other men at the reunion—but Emily seemed to enjoy it all the same.

"Thanks," she said sheepishly. "And you looked just smashing in that suit. I didn't even realize you owned a suit."

"Very funny. In fact, I own several, and some really nice wide-striped ties, too, a nice authentic polyester blend."

She laughed, turned away from the suitcase without the T-shirt she'd been hunting for, and leaned up against the dresser. "Thanks for the compliment. It helps."

He got off the bed and walked toward the TV again. "You looked a little off-balance all night, but you shouldn't have. You haven't done anything but change for the better."

She looked down at the carpet. This was Marty's heart talking, not his eyes, and they both knew it. He was treading that dangerous line between gentlemanly chivalry and single-minded flattery.

"Marty, why hasn't some nice girl snagged you up yet?" She looked up, right into his eyes, and he blushed this time.

"You're kidding, right? Me? The independently wealthy Wal-Mart manager from Lancaster? I haven't met a girl yet stupid enough to fall for that one."

He walked past the TV and over to her.

"Are you calling me stupid?"

He laughed. "No, you dope."

"So now I'm a dope."

He stood there for a long moment, not moving, not remembering where they'd been all evening, and not daring to think where they were going after this moment. Emily looked up at him and saw that he was already looking at her, a flushed, confused sort of look in his eyes. This was the look of unplanned, unrehearsed emotion, and she matched his gaze with her own version.

They stared at each other, searching for questions a moment longer, and then Marty timidly opened his arms and stood next to her with his arms outstretched. She slipped into his arms and he enfolded her in his embrace.

11

M RS. DAISY HENDERSON WAS PRAYING AGAIN, and an astute observer might almost have seen drops of blood on her forehead from the fervor of it.

Although her name suited her, Daisy had never really liked it much. As a young slip of a schoolgirl many decades ago she hadn't minded the name, daisies being such bright, cheery flowers. The street side of their frame bungalow had overflowed with delicate ivory daisies every year, and to this day they reminded her of her mother, who had tended them lovingly.

But an increasingly independent young woman named Daisy Mae McCartney hadn't appreciated being saddled with such a frivolous name. She'd yearned for a no-nonsense, take-charge name like Jane or Doris or even the more mysterious Chloe. No one would take a silly little thing named Daisy Mae very seriously. And perhaps they hadn't. But God did.

She married Dale Henderson, four years her senior, in 1955. Things had certainly changed in the world since those days, but back then Daisy knew a woman of little means and a lot of gumption could turn her life around by marrying the right man. Dale Henderson was as close to a knight in shining armor as Daisy could have hoped, and their thirty years together had been blissfully happy ones surrounded by friends and loved ones, except for one small hitch. They hadn't had any children. In lesser marriages this sort of strain might have led to acrimony, mutual blame, and eventually divorce, but in Dale and Daisy's case it somehow kept them close. Without children to distract them from each other, their relationship blossomed like the side yard at her mother's house, happy and sunny despite the quiet anguish of Daisy's maternal heart. If God had seen fit to deny her children, He had at least given her a doting husband with whom she could share her sorrow.

Amid her pain during those childless years, Daisy learned to pray. Her own disappointments about barrenness taught her the quickness and openness with which she approached her God, praying for her own needs. And her tender heart and sharp attention to detail taught her to pray for others with the clout of someone who understood suffering on a more profound level. Despite her best efforts to keep her conversations with God private, by the time she was thirty she'd been accurately deemed a prayer warrior by anyone who knew her.

At eighty, she now brought this same clout to her urgent prayers for Emily Saunders. Over the past few years Daisy had sensed within Emily a wash of pain that she could not fully grasp. Her own widowhood at age fifty had been devastating; it seemed impossible to envision Emily's grief as a much younger widow with two small children to rear. Last month's mugging had left even the most devout in the congregation shaken and perplexed, as if God must have mistaken Emily for someone else that night. Today's news of a resulting pregnancy was surely one more cruel blow in a seemingly unending series of devastations in her short life.

And so, with this posture toward the long-suffering Emily, Daisy entered into yet another brow-furrowing dialogue with her God.

+ + + + +

ALAN WARD LOOKED FORWARD to Five-Hundred Rummy nights with his grandson. The tradition had started a few years earlier when grandson Paul Dobson, then ten, contracted the mumps—right in the middle of the school year, much to the consternation of his hard-working, day-job parents. Alan eagerly offered to watch Paul during the day while his daughter, Celia Ward Dobson, and Paul's father, George Dobson, were both at work.

During the first day of Paul's confinement, he slept through the morning and spent much of the afternoon complaining that his throat felt swollen and lumpy. Grandpa Alan quipped that they should have called it the lumps instead of the mumps, and Paul snorted a laugh in spite of himself.

"You're funny, Grandpa."

"Funny-lookin', maybe."

Paul smiled again. "It's not really so bad ... for a disease. It's mostly just crummy, but Mom says I might get to stay home from school the rest of the week." He beamed at the prospect of a week in pajamas playing video games and eating applesauce with cinnamon.

"The whole week?" Alan gasped, feigning surprise. "What will the two of us find to do together for a whole week?"

"I dunno, Grandpa. Maybe play more Mario Kart?" Paul asked hopefully.

"No," Alan protested, "that's too easy. It's like cheating."

"Cheating? How?"

"You don't really have to do anything. You don't have to think. I have a better idea for us." He stood and walked to the coat rack where his cardigan was draped over one of the already-overcrowded pegs. Reaching exaggeratedly in his pocket, as if he couldn't locate the desired item, he rolled his eyes toward Paul and hung his tongue out of his mouth in cartoon fashion. Paul, his curiosity obviously piqued, waited to see what bit of excitement his grandpa would come up with next.

Alan dramatically pulled a deck of ordinary playing cards out of the left pocket and held the cards aloft. He could see Paul's disappointment and sighed at the current generation's inability to find excitement and pleasure in the simple things.

"Is that it, Grandpa? A deck of cards?"

"Is that it? *Is that it?*" Alan replied, sounding more shocked than dismayed. "Why, young man, you're looking at the video games of my day. This is what we did for fun—and we had a lot of fun, let me tell you."

He strode to the coffee table next to the couch where Paul was reclining in his pajamas, wrapped in the granny-square afghan Alan's late wife had crocheted twenty years earlier. Paul instinctively moved his feet to allow Alan to sit at the other end of the couch, and Alan sat forcefully, leaning in and placing the deck firmly on Paul's end of the coffee table.

"Do you know how to shuffle a deck?" Alan asked his young captive pupil.

Paul's eyebrows wrinkled into a skeptical frown. "No, but so what?" His eyes met Alan's. "Do you?"

Alan grinned. "I thought you'd never ask."

Opening the paper box with one hand and sliding the entire deck into the palm of his other hand, Alan deftly shuffled the deck on the coffee table with a flutter of cards and a flourish of fingers. Paul listened to the quiet whoosh of cards rustling from Alan's arched thumbs to his waiting fingers beneath. Alan noted his grandson watching him intently. An unrehearsed smile slipped across Paul's face while he wasn't guarding it, and Alan took it all in.

"Now, m'boy," he announced to Paul as he began dealing first a card to Paul and then one to himself. "Let's play a little game I like to call Five-Hundred Rummy."

Paul pulled himself more upright at his end of the couch, his entire torso slipping out from under the familial protection of Gramma Cissy's afghan. "Grandpa, wow, you're a real card fish!"

Alan laughed, knowing he meant "cardsharp."

"Card *shark*, Paul—I'm a card shark. Now, pay attention, 'cause here are the rules ..."

+ + + + +

WHEN ALAN ARRIVED AT CELIA AND GEORGE'S HOUSE this particular night for Five-Hundred Rummy—for what had to be the five-hundredth time—Celia answered the door looking distraught and out of sorts. He entered swiftly, hung his coat on the rack easily with one hand, and moved in next to his daughter, putting both now-free arms around her.

"Cel, honey, what's the matter? Is everyone all right?" Alan began to look around the living room and into the dining room, eyes searching for George and Paul. Seeing them both in the background, going about their business of prepping the dining room table for lengthy card game play—snacks, drinks, more snacks, and a single deck of good playing cards—Alan turned his attention back to Celia in his arms. "What's happened?"

She leaned in to him and sighed. "It's Emily Saunders. Did you hear what happened to her?"

Perhaps she was referring to the mugging, but that was last month. Dear Lord, what else could have happened to that woman now?

"No, what now?" Alan asked.

"She's pregnant."

Alan's reaction was instant and confused. "She's what?" he blurted out loudly.

"Pregnant," Celia repeated more softly. "Isn't it just the worst?"

"The poor woman."

Celia nodded. Alan continued with his train of thought.

"Honestly, though, I would have thought better of Peter. Taking advantage of the poor woman in the vulnerable state she's been in the past few years."

Celia stopped nodding suddenly and fixed a perplexed gaze on her father. "What are you talking about, Peter taking advantage of her? When?"

Alan frowned. "Well, getting her pregnant. Why? What are *you* talking about?"

"The attack—the rape, of course ..."

The two of them eyed each other suspiciously, until separate realizations dawned on each of them. They talked over one another trying to get their incredulity out.

"You thought she was raped?"

"You thought it was Peter?"

Alan and Celia looked at each other for an interminable moment, neither willing to break the silence. Alan finally spoke.

"So tell me, what happened?"

"She got sick during the C.E. meeting the other night. Everett thought—well, *everyone* thought—she had the flu. Turns out it was morning sickness ... at night, I guess." She shook her head in disbelief.

"How did everyone figure it out?"

"She came right out and said it—trying to calm everyone down that she didn't have the flu. Honestly, I don't think she really meant to say it like that, Dad, but Everett was making a big stink about her giving us all the flu and everything—"

"And she mentioned the attack then?" Alan surmised.

"Well, no, she didn't get that far. She was probably so embarrassed about getting sick, and then about having told everyone like that, that she just left the meeting before we got anything done."

"So, she mentioned the attack later then? To Meg maybe?" Alan offered, his mind still not wrapped around how the puzzle pieces all fit together.

"No, not then either, that I know of. I guess we all just assumed it, since it was over a month ago and all."

Alan nodded.

"The idea that it could be Peter never even occurred to me till now, really. Probably didn't occur to anyone else, either."

"Of course not," Alan offered. "Why should it? It must've been the attack. Right, yes, you're right. I didn't put two and two together, that's all," he mumbled, trying to convince himself more than Celia.

"Dad, you don't really think that Peter—"

"Nooo," he interrupted graciously. "Not at all. I just wasn't thinking right. Don't worry about it, Cel. Forget I said it. I don't want to get that poor girl in any more trouble than she's already in."

Celia nodded, hugging her father and sighing out her frustration. "It's all so terrible, you know?"

"I know, sweetie."

He looked over her shoulder to see Paul seated at the dining room table in his lucky chair, shuffling the deck with ease and eyeing the other three spots at the table with a particular amount of anticipation. "Grandpa, you gotta come cut the cards!"

Celia broke free of her father's embrace and looked at him for reassurance.

"She'll be fine, Celia. We'll all be there for her. You worry too much."

Celia smiled weakly. Alan pointed past her to her son.

"Now, let's go whoop some preteen ass at Rummy, shall we?"

+ + + + +

If Janie Newman thought her husband functioned amazingly well on two-thirds of the sleep she herself needed, she would have reconsidered her position upon seeing him the morning after Monday night's Christian education meeting. The fiasco with Emily Saunders—her outburst about the pregnancy—had cost him the entire meeting and he was still fuming. Once Emily hurriedly left the meeting after announcing her delicate condition, Everett had tried to corral the faithful and get the meeting to order. They needed to make decisions about the new Sunday School curriculum in time to order it and couldn't afford to lose the whole night to a relational gaffe by the committee's most irresponsible member. But it wasn't going to happen. The stunned were too much in shock to continue, and the gossips—often self-disguised as "prayer warriors"—were too eager to peddle their new information along the prayer phone tree.

This was almost worse than Emily ruining a regular meeting by disagreeing with him at every turn. Last night's stunt had derailed the committee and might end up forcing them to postpone the beginning of the next quarter if the curriculum didn't arrive in time.

To keep from disturbing Janie's precarious sleep, Everett had not gone to bed at all last night. He'd stayed up to pace the floor of the family room and think. Around three in the morning he began to weary of the task and succumbed to the La-Z-Boy nestled in the far corner, grabbing the TV's remote control and heading straight for the History Channel. A show about Civil War reenactments lulled him into a fitful, haunted sleep.

At nine he stepped into the kitchen and smelled no coffee, heard no rustling anywhere in the house.

"Janie!" he called, his need to have his sounding board at his side overpowering his usual sense of decorum regarding his wife's sleep. "Janie, are you up? I need to talk to you!"

He listened quietly, finally hearing the sound he wanted: Janie's slippered feet in the hallway. Her sweet humming was missing today. Last night's disaster had affected her as well, but probably only through him. She rounded the corner and was standing in the kitchen, tying her flannel robe snugly at her trim waist.

"Yes, dear?" she asked, anticipating the conversation and dutifully accepting her place in it—not looking up from her robe, not wanting to make eye contact just yet.

He strode to her and grasped her arms firmly. She looked up at him sweetly and fought back a yawn, and he found he didn't have the heart to put her through another of his personal tirades about Christian education and Emily Saunders.

"Nothing, Janie. I was just upset about last night's meeting. About what happened with Emily. I never get a break with that woman around."

"Sweetheart, look at it from Emily's point of view. She's got to be crushed to find this out now. You can't make everything about you, dear."

He let go of her arms and turned toward the kitchen counter. Janie was wrong. This was about him. More than she would ever know.

+ + + + +

It was only Tuesday and Pastor Ray Compton had already logged more phone time for the day than he sometimes did for an entire week. In the past twenty-four hours he'd begun to rethink getting call-waiting in the church office. He'd never get done talking to people if he didn't have an excuse to cut one person off in favor of the next one. Church members who were at the Christian education meeting the night before began calling him as soon as they got home. In fact, judging from the timing, some of them had probably dialed up their cell phones while they were still in the church parking lot. Motives were difficult to judge in a situation such as this, especially since Emily Saunders had long been a source of controversy, speculation, and gossip. It had started with the death of her husband a few years ago and continued with her relationship with the perpetually single Peter Bellows, and more recently, her mugging while out of town at her high school reunion. The latest news coming to him from all quarters—except from Emily herself—was that she was now pregnant.

Ray sighed and relaxed into the high-backed chair behind his desk, grateful for a few moments without a phone ringing in his ear. This whole situation had "professional therapist" written all over it, a thought that made him feel guilty. He had no wish to write off Emily in her time of greatest need, but he also knew that she was now juggling more than he could expect anyone to handle. His expertise and strengths lay with marriage and family counseling. Run-of-the-mill family counseling. Wayward teens, bored housewives, overworked husbands. Reaching out to someone whom God had chosen to sling all over the relational mat seemed too precarious for Ray. It wasn't that he wanted to shirk his responsibilities or that he didn't take Emily's situation seriously. Quite the contrary: he took her situation so seriously that he didn't want to risk screwing her up for life with platitudinous advice that would have to come from outside his own years of counseling experience.

It was quite a pastoral dilemma, really.

He plucked his Bible off the book hutch just above his desk and thumbed deftly to the book of Job. Eventually, the call from Emily would come—and if it didn't come by tomorrow morning, he'd call her himself. When they talked, he needed to be ready. Rereading this book of the Bible—and maybe playing a few psalm tapes—would help him get into her situation a little more empathetically. Wanting to have a few reliable names ready to pass along to Emily, he scribbled on a notepad next to his keyboard: "Call drs. in morning." He would have to make a few phone calls of his own.

As he mused further, the desk phone near his left hand rang, and he jolted a little. Taking a deep breath, he lifted the receiver to his ear with a tentative, "Hello?"

The welcome voice of his wife, Holly, replied. "Ray, Peter Bellows was just here looking for you."

"At the house?"

"Yes. I told him your Tuesday hours at the church were in the afternoon, and he turned tail and left. I'm guessing he's on his way over there now."

"You didn't get to talk to him at all? Was Emily with him?"

"No, she wasn't with him. And no, I didn't get even a peep out of him about her. He was focused on finding you."

He heard her sigh into the phone. She had probably been fielding calls at home all afternoon.

"When was he there? When did he leave there?" Ray glanced at his watch, hoping to calculate accurately when to expect Peter.

"He left here no more than five minutes ago. I really couldn't have talked to him anyway. The kids are due home from play practice any minute. I called you as soon as he left. I figured you'd want to know he's on his way over, so you could be sure to not be busy when he shows up."

"Okay. That works. I'll clear the decks here and wait for him."

Holly sighed again. "Just be careful, Ray. I don't know how much Peter knows. Or if he's even talked to Emily yet."

"True. I hadn't thought of that. He could be coming over here looking for confirmation of what he's heard."

"Has Emily talked to you herself yet?"

"No. I made a mental note to call her by tomorrow morning if I hadn't heard from her first. It seemed better to let her work up the nerve to call me on her own. She's gotta be scared out of her wits about all this."

"Good plan," Holly agreed. "But I wish you'd heard from Emily. It'd be easier to help Peter if you knew more first-hand."

"Wait, that's right. He's not on the committee anymore, is he? That means he didn't hear it from Emily last night at the meeting like everyone else."

"Poor Peter."

"This situation keeps getting more complicated." Ray's voice softened a little, a resigned quality to it that he knew Holly would pick up on.

"Ray, you just talk to Peter as best you can, offer him a place to vent. That might be all he needs right now."

"He'll need to come clean about everything at some point, and the sooner he does that, the better."

"Come clean? About what?"

"Well, about the pregnancy, of course."

There was a palpable silence on Holly's end of the phone. "Ray, what *are* you talking about?"

"Peter and Emily. The premarital sex. You know."

"I know of no such thing, Ray Compton, and you'd better be careful who you tell that atrocious story." Holly sounded positively perturbed.

"What are *you* talking about?" he asked his wife in return.

"It's obvious that she's pregnant because of her attack last month. It was obviously a rape, Ray."

The silence now extended from his end of the phone.

"Are you sure about this?"

"Well, it just makes sense, that's all."

"But it could be Peter."

She sighed. "I suppose it could. If you're inclined to think that way."

"Holly, you know I'm not like that. It's another possible explanation, though."

She said nothing.

"Oh, and Holly?"

"Yes?"

"After this is all over, remind me to apply for that job at McDonald's, okay?"

She laughed in spite of herself. "Sure thing, sweets." She made kissing noises into the phone and hung up.

Ray eased the phone back into the cradle, and through the silence he heard Peter's Ford Bronco pull into the church lot outside his office window. As he heard the truck door slam and Peter's feet scuffle across the gravel in the lot, the phone rang. He looked from the door that was about to open to the phone in its cradle signaling yet another incoming call. The office door swung open on its hinges after one perfunctory rap, and Peter Bellows strode in, looking confused and yet somehow still undaunted.

Ray turned to Peter and away from the phone, which rang three more times and then went silent as the caller was automatically transferred over to the church's voice mail.

At the other end of the phone, Emily Saunders was sobbing, frustrated at not getting through to Ray all morning long and yet guiltily relieved that she wouldn't have to sniffle her way through another phone call like yesterday's call to Marty. She hung up without leaving a message.

12

WIDOWHOOD NEVER AGREED WITH ME. In that first year after Jonathan died, life was filled with little more than strange ironies—as if God were telling bad puns or something. Other women in my congregation got engaged, got hitched, bore offspring like rabbits. The women's fellowship study couldn't hold my attention during that first year, and despite much wise counsel to the contrary, I left the group and never went back. I had become a fluke, an unintended outcast within the family of God, and absolutely everything anyone said to me was glib, glib, glib. My battle cry became "You don't understand," and I alienated more than one good friend who took me seriously when I foolishly asked to be left alone. I didn't want to be surrounded by gawking, ingratiating friends; I didn't need them. The one person who could have helped me deal with the severity of God's sovereignty in those early days had been taken from me. What kind of sick joke was this? God was nothing more than an abusive father. And yet, with a sickening ache in the pit of my stomach, I'd fling myself back into His arms again and again, alternately hating what He had done to me, yet realizing that I had nowhere else to turn.

The second year was a little less of an emotional drain, but time slowed to a crawl, and I felt the seconds of my life tick away methodically, one after another. Millions of dirty dishes and clothes, innumerable runny noses, skinned knees and quarrels, countless grocery shopping trips—each was an exercise in patience, diligence, and concentrated effort. The small decisions that make up a life became unbearably important, and I often feared that a poorly made minor decision might lead to a major calamity. Deep down, I believed that time would heal my wound, and so I was glad to be rid of the creeping hours and days. Their passing signaled yet another step on the interminable road to recovery. But, I was also aware of the fact that I was past thirty, and that I had very little to show for it. I had no husbandly laurels upon which to rest my head, and had never really had any of my own, either. So, I was paradoxically grieved at the irretrievable loss of time.

It felt as if I was waiting for Jonathan to get home late from work, so that we could start our evening together as a family. I was waiting around for someone to show up, for something to happen, so that I could say to myself, "Okay, now we're all here. Let's get going." Lately it alarmed me to think that Peter Bellows might now be the person I was waiting for. It had little to do with Peter himself. I suppose I would have been equally concerned about any man who showed up in my life. The shock lay not in who Peter was, but in who he wasn't. He wasn't Jonathan. The thought of struggling to get to know a man from scratch all over again intimidated me. I had learned an obvious fact: death puts a real damper on romance.

✦ ✦ ✦ ✦ ✦

THAT FIRST NIGHT BACK IN PITTSBURGH after the attack, after the kids and I had sat on the couch all evening, hugging and cuddling, so happy to be touching each other again, I reluctantly took one of the pills the doctor prescribed to help me get some sleep. I climbed the familiar stairs, threw on the T-shirt I sleep in, and crawled bone-weary

into the middle of the big bed. As I felt the drug tickle my consciousness with its magic, I thought I was headed for a dreamless oblivion. I
didn't think I was ripe for a bad dream.

+ + + + +

IN THE DREAM I AM NOWHERE IN PARTICULAR. I tug the rope over my
head and fiddle with it as though it were a necklace. Footsteps shuffle
behind me, and the flimsy dinette chair is wrenched out from under
my feet in a sudden jerk. My feet plunge down toward the floor, but
miss it by inches as the nylon rope around my neck overtakes itself
running upward, interrupted in its mad dash by the fleshy part of my
throat, which constricts freakishly.

My legs twist uncontrollably in the air, which only pulls my
weight further downward. I try to take some air into my lungs, past
the grasping rope, but the gulp lodges in my throat, and cords whisk
the breath back up and out of my open mouth. I gasp a burp and
the bitter taste of bile rises up through the threadlike opening of my
windpipe and into my mouth.

My hands instinctively go to my throat, trying to wrench the rope
back and over my chin as I feel rope burns twist their hairs of pain
into my neck. I get two fingers from each hand between the rope and
the flesh on my neck, and I gobble down a single bubble of air before
the rope adapts its tightness to this new shape and clutches once more.
The slight inrush of air keeps me from blacking out for only a few moments longer, and I sense my body beginning to surrender.

My feet are now swaying uneasily to and fro, punctuated inter-
mittently by the involuntary twitching of one foot, then the other.
My fingers yield inside the noose but I can't withdraw them. The rope
scorches more than ever.

A cluster of starry, fluorescent pinpoints of light explode in front
of me like mute fireworks, each erupting and then sinking into its
own black hole, drawing me down, down, still farther down, and yet
away, away, distantly away. I try to shriek, but my outcry is strangled

by the omnipresent grasp of the rope on my throat. My body lurches in a violent, spasmodic jerk.

+ + + + +

I AWOKE SUDDENLY, drenched in another of my now-famous night sweats. That night at the reunion led to more damage than I apparently cared to acknowledge. At least while I was awake.

13

"The Christian may walk with unbelievers in seeking the good of society, but his chief motive should be the glory of God. Christians should avoid any voluntary association in which they cannot maintain a consistent testimony for Christ."

> —*Testimony* of the Reformed Presbyterian Church
> of North America, 16:4

I HAD REACHED UP TO PUT MY ARMS AROUND MARTY'S NECK and clasped my hands behind his head, turning my face up to meet his. Instead of looking at each other for confirmation of what to do or not do next, I pulled his face down to mine without much effort, and our lips touched. He pulled me still closer, almost engulfing me in his arms, with a determined force that surprised me. He too seemed taken aback for a moment, and then suddenly the next decision was made and we were really kissing for the first time.

In the back of my mind I knew that, if this had started in the hotel hallway with one of us fumbling with a key in the lock, things would have gone no further than that kiss. If there had been any interruption at all—any time to make one more conscious decision about what we were doing—the whole escapade would have ground to a halt.

But for some inexplicable reason, God held the outside world at arm's length. Before long, my racing thoughts guided my hands, first down his back, then grabbing at random buttons on his shirt, then both hands were in his hair trying to pull his head closer to mine. I missed this, ached for it—and wasn't I sensing the same yearning in Marty?

I felt too much the aggressor and pulled back slightly. In response, Marty shoved me down onto the bed, kissing me frantically and fumbling with the buttons on my dress. I reached one hand up to help him, but he pushed it away, mumbling "No." I'm still not sure just how long all our grasping at buttons and zippers lasted. The whole time I was expecting to hear the phone ring, the doorbell buzz, *something* to stop this insanity. A small, panicked part of me cried out for a diversion. But none came. We seemed to have been left alone with our sin.

At one point Marty buried his head in my neck and repeatedly gasped something in my ear. He caught his breath, and then I could make out what he had been trying to say: "No ... no ... *no* ..."

And just that suddenly, it was all over. His heart was beating madly; in contrast, mine had slowed to a heavy, dull pounding that I felt at every pulse point. I felt warm perspiration trickle from his temple onto mine.

Without warning, Marty broke free of my grasp and got up. I opened my eyes and saw him turn away from me. I lay there and watched him get dressed—exposed, bitter and ashamed. I yanked the end of the bedspread over me and stared at the ceiling. Marty sat back down on the edge of the bed, but didn't turn to me or speak. Already I'd forgotten what he felt like, smelled like—the wisps were all gone. Marty bent down to pick up his shirt and shoes, and then stood up, still not facing me. He grabbed his keys off the dresser, looked at himself momentarily in the mirror, shook his head, and stepped away from me toward the door.

"Wait," I said weakly, not sure what, if anything, I had left to offer him to make him stay.

"What?" he asked flatly, pulling his shirt on.

My blood ran cold. "Stay here."

"Here? Tonight?"

"Yeah. Please?"

He turned to face me, finally, and when I saw the defeated look in his eyes, I instantly wished he hadn't turned around, but had simply walked out the door and never come back.

"You gotta be kidding." It wasn't meant as a nasty put-down, but as a simple statement. I already knew that lingering, wallowing here in this stupidity was about as appropriate as two thieves robbing a bank and then sitting outside on the front steps fondling the money. Now I was asking him to go back in and steal the loose change, too.

The steel door shut with a heavy thud, and I heard Marty let himself into the room next to mine. I heard the television go on, heard Marty toss things across the room at the wall adjoining mine—his keys?—and then heard the shower running. I buried my face in the pillow and bawled like a baby.

14

"As there is no sin so small, but it deserves damnation, so there is no sin so great, that it can bring damnation upon those who truly repent."

— *The Westminster Confession of Faith*, 15:4

SOMETIME WHILE IT WAS STILL DARK I AWOKE, probably not much later, feeling mummified in the warm bedspread, the pillowcase still damp under my cheek. I didn't remember turning off the light by the bed, but it was off now. Lying motionless on the bed, I listened for noise from the outside world. I thought I heard a faint murmur coming from Marty's room next door. Curiosity and guilt got the better of me: I just had to hear what someone with enough conscience to keep him from sleeping did so soon after so great a sin, besides take a shower.

I pulled myself up to the headboard of the bed and sat up, feeling quite like a mermaid with my legs encased tightly in the covers. I felt a sudden draft, and tried to close the front of my gaping dress, remembering that all three buttons were somewhere on the floor.

Pressing my ear up against the wall, I heard the television in Marty's room, and with some concentration made out Marty's lone voice, speaking low but heatedly.

"Who could he be calling at this hour?" I wondered aloud, and my heartbeat quickened. I began cataloging all the possible recipients of the private information he was obviously sharing. Hank? No. His mother? Please, God, no. Some friend I'd never met? This seemed the only comforting answer, so I made it the truth for now.

In an effort to reestablish some semblance of communication, no matter how pathetic, I rapped on the wall three times and waited. Marty broke off in mid-conversation, and the world was suspended in silence for a moment. I scarcely breathed, hoping against hope that I'd hear him hang up the phone and come running from his room over to mine, pounding on the door, pleading for us to stop this foolishness and be reconciled. Instead, all I heard was one disturbingly loud thud on the wall in response. I threw the pillow back across my face hastily to keep me from crying out, as if Marty had walloped me and not the wall. The reverberation died inside my head, and Marty was still silent. I heard him get off the bed, but he didn't come knocking at my door. The drone of the television snapped off, and I heard his bed groan as he returned to it.

I lay there, perplexed and silent, waiting for something to happen. When it became obvious by the suffocating silence in the room that Marty had probably fallen asleep and nothing was going to happen any time soon, I switched on the lamp on the nightstand and climbed off the bed. Gravity pulled the bedspread off my legs and down to my ankles, and I stepped out of it, walking over to the open suitcase on the dresser. I grabbed the oversized T-shirt I had worn the other two nights and draped it over the lid of the suitcase along with a pair of sweats. The wrinkled, damaged dress fell off my shoulders and to the floor. Bending down to pick it up, I found one of the three buttons at the foot of the bed and put both the dress and the button in the suitcase.

I looked up from the suitcase and saw myself in the mirror. There I stood: no clothing but my camisole; hair sticking out every which way; necklace backwards, cascading down my back instead of down the front; black mascara smudged in large circles under my eyes as if I had not slept for a week; the end of my hoop earring hooked inside my ear. Earring? One? The other must have come out while I slept. I closed my eyes, hoisting the flimsy camisole over my head and pulling the T-shirt over my body before daring to open my eyes again. I was painfully grateful for the T-shirt's ability to cover up everything in one fell swoop. Everything but my face, I realized. *And that's the naked part.*

As I pulled on the sweats, I felt the events of that night begin to crowd their way inside my head, parading themselves in front of me rapidly as if to say, "Why didn't you see this coming? It was obvious this was where you were headed."

I was not ready for this—not ready for that painful first step of repentance that follows on the heels of regret. Right now, some basic, necessary ablutions were needed to clear my head for the heart-wrenching episode that was rushing in on me. Padding to the bathroom sink, I ran the water as hot as I felt I could endure it and cupped my hands to catch some of it. I bent low over the sink and thrust my face into my palms and held it there till much of the water had seeped through my fingers. The water dripped out of my eyes and I pulled the stopper closed, watching the sink quickly fill with steamy water. The spigot closed off easily and I took in a gasp of air and plunged my face down into the water. The heat of the water stung my face, the edges of skin where the water and air met feeling almost unbearable. I held my face under the water, eyes tightly shut, for as long as I could stand it—fifteen seconds at most—and then raised my head out of the water, gasping and feeling fiery wet heat under my skin and a moist brisk draft just on the surface.

Turning to sit on the toilet, I felt water now dripping onto my sweats. I didn't get up until my face had nearly dried, preferring instead to sit lifelessly and let my bizarre thoughts wander aimlessly for a bit. God's justice was beginning to catch up with me; accountability was at hand. As if preprogrammed, still relatively detached from the impending wave of guilt, I stood and walked to the bed, where I noiselessly climbed in and pulled the sheet up to my waist. I sat silently for a while, knowing that God's tap-on-the-shoulder was due any moment now.

For a few quiet, deathly still moments nothing happened. I was almost relieved to feel nothing, to have this long interlude to gather up my fortitude and brace myself for what was coming.

Then it hit. The crushed look in Marty's eyes after he got off the bed loomed large in front of me, caricatured larger than life now, and I couldn't stand it anymore. It was ruined. It was all over. I was absolutely certain that decades of intense friendship now meant nothing. It had always been the one relationship I could count on all those years, even in the long absence, knowing in the back of my mind full well that, if I ever needed him and called for him, he'd have come running. It was this subconscious thought that had gotten me through more bad times than I probably knew. But, at this moment, sitting on the hotel bed half-naked, realizing that things would never be the same no matter how much patching we did, I truly understood how much our relationship had shaped who I had become.

These were frightening moments more so than sad ones, because I had inadvertently allowed a non-Christian to become closer to my heart in many ways than even my husband had been while he was alive. I had never realized it, would never have understood it even if I had been confronted with it at the time, but now it was obvious.

My occasional anger with Marty over his religious pigheadedness was really anger that he wasn't willing to convert for the sake of what might have been. Granted, I wasn't willing to "convert" either, but in the early days I was always waiting for his chivalry to get the better of him, for him to rescue me from the boyfriends who weren't as right for me as he was, who never stood a chance of knowing me the way he did. And, sitting here alone in the silence, I again blamed him for not just giving in and seeing things my way.

I wondered if Marty had ever felt the same way about me. Surely he had, since I knew his feelings for me were always skating on the edge of romance, and that he had more than once seen fit to remind me of my own stubbornness in matters of God. Some of our classmates might have said the ending to this evening was something they had seen coming for a long time, and most of them would probably have smiled slyly if they were to find out, thinking we had finally come to our senses and seen how right we were for each other. But all the encounter had done, really, was to tear a mile-wide chasm between Marty and me.

As I felt my throat tighten with emotion, I remembered the chasm had always been there; we just weren't willing to acknowledge its presence. Friendship was never enough. So what remained? Hopelessly alone, I realized nothing remained. I could think of little else in my life with any sense of joy as I felt Marty slip out of my soul, out of my heart, and onto the floor, lost somewhere with the other two buttons from my dress.

✛ ✛ ✛ ✛ ✛

TEARS FOLLOWED, MANY OF THEM. I held my face in my hands and sobbed openly, audibly. At first I was concerned that the noise might awaken Marty, and that his chivalrous nature would kick in and make him come over to see if I was all right. Suddenly I had hit the point on the path to repentance where the last thing I wanted was to be interrupted. I tried to muffle my sobs enough that I could continue and finish what I had started.

"God," I began, mostly to myself, "I'm sorry, I'm sorry, I'm *so* sorry." I immediately felt worse. That was how I knew He heard me.

"I didn't know this was gonna happen. I didn't plan it. I didn't. It just happened. I'm sorry, I'm sorry."

And I sobbed a little more and thought a disturbing thought, one that rang true: I had known. I saw it coming. I could have stopped it.

I stretched out my legs in front of me and lay prostrate on the bed, face down, covers wrapping my legs again. "Forgive me," I cried.

Nothing. Silence. Silence from Marty next door and, I thought, from God as well. The former relieved me; the latter terrified me. Why wasn't God patting me on the back and telling me everything would be all right? The situation reminded me of the early days after my husband's death, when God was just silent enough to make a point: Shut up, I'm here. Cease striving and know that I am God, you big maroon.

I swallowed a sob and lay quietly on the bed, waiting for answers like a Pentecostal waits for tongues. But I couldn't will the answers to appear. Perhaps, as with Jonathan's death, they wouldn't appear anytime soon, perhaps not ever. But this had a purpose; of that much I was certain. That one fact had gotten me through everything up until this point—the consoling, comforting fact of God's ultimate sovereignty and control. Nothing else would have been able to help me handle much of what I had been through.

+ + + + +

MY MIND WANDERED FROM GOD TO MARTY for a moment. The encounter had been intense, short, and almost violent, something I had never experienced with Jonathan. For one thing, the impending guilt had kept Marty and I rushing to stay ahead of it, something I had never had to deal with while married. Ten seconds of clear thought from either one of us would have made the difference, but we really had made sure with our actions that those ten seconds never appeared.

With Marty I was utterly alone, and I had never felt so much like myself, and that was certainly not a good thing. With this outrageous leap of logic, I was sure that something like this would sway Marty away from his annoying habit of insisting that mankind was inherently good, that I was always making this big deal out of my "sins." Didn't Marty now understand his own sinfulness? Surely he could no longer deny the powerful, deep-rooted effects of sin.

But here I was, having mused my way out of a contrite and repentant posture of heart and into a mental seminary debate with Marty again, and he wasn't even here. God deserved an apology for being pa-

tiently silent throughout the entire thought-episode while I tried to regain my sense of prayerful vigilance. I began to wonder if I hadn't lost it
entirely when I thought of Peter, who was across the state with my kids.
So there's the rub, I thought bitterly. How irreparable was the damage to
that relationship now, or would I end up compounding the problem by
not telling him what had happened? He was a good judge of character,
though; he'd know something was wrong. I'd have to tell him.

Was I willing to sacrifice the relationship I had with Peter? It
seemed a moot point; it wasn't my decision now, but his. I already felt
like used merchandise with him, wondering how he ever entertained
the thought of inheriting an instant family with me and the kids.
But, I knew he entertained that very thought, for such was the way in
our circles. Help her with some yard work; baby-sit the kids once or
twice; sit with her in church for at least four weeks in a row; remember
everyone's birthdays; invite her to all the church social functions (and
maybe one or two things wholly outside the confines of the church,
like the sing-along of Handel's *Messiah* in Heinz Hall at Christmas)—
and then, pow! You ask her to marry you, and she says yes, and down
the aisle you go hopping, with a new toaster and a blender and lots of
nice handmade cross-stitching of Bible quotations under your arms.
And you live happily ever after, and she heaves a sigh of relief that her
poor children have another stable father figure, a job she was failing
miserably at anyway.

+ + + + +

"I'M SORRY, LORD," I SAID AGAIN, realizing for a second time that I had
interrupted my penitent prayers with peripheral reflections on my life.
"Please keep me close to You through all this. Help me to think Your
thoughts after You." Then other thoughts came. *His* thoughts, diverse
yet coherent when taken as a whole.

Cease striving and know that I am God.

*I am the Lord your God, who brought you out of the land of Egypt,
out of the house of slavery. You shall have no other gods before Me.*

I the Lord your God am a jealous God.

What is man, so frail and weak, that You should remember him?

For the guilt that binds us is our own, arising from our own sin, leaving us without the will or the capacity to do good....

+ + + + +

IT WAS STILL PITCH-BLACK WHEN I WOKE from a fitful sleep, T-shirt and sweats keeping me warm in lieu of a blanket. The air felt suffocating and stifling. Restlessness got the better of me and I grabbed my sneakers from under the chair and slipped them on.

A short walk in the dead quiet of night—the fresh crisp air, the blackness—would surely do me a world of good. Grabbing my purse and the room key and throwing on a sweatshirt, I walked through the empty hotel lobby and out the front door, heading around the back near the river, where I would be found nearly three days later, memories damaged but remorse firmly intact.

15

J ANIE NEWMAN SOMETIMES WONDERED what was behind those ha-
zel eyes of Everett's. There were times she came into the study and
caught him staring. Not out the large, curved bay window—which
would have made its own sense and not been something to notice—but
out into nothing, right in front of him. She could tell he wasn't thinking about anything important, wasn't planning the next day or the next
church meeting. He wasn't thinking anything at all at those times, and
it seemed as if he had been sitting there for ages like that. And that truly
frightened her. She never, though, mentioned it to Everett.

It was happening more frequently lately; that was the scary part.
He'd gone on a business trip to Easton a month or more ago, and in
the week before the trip he'd had one of his blank-out episodes every
day, at nearly the same time each day. He didn't talk much about the
trip, was almost secretive about it, in fact. It would have worried her
more, if it hadn't been silly to imagine an electrical engineer being
secretive about the specifics of his work with his wife, who only knew
enough about electricity to turn on a wall switch or use the microwave
to reheat leftovers. Still, it felt odd to watch Everett skulk around
the house obsessively packing and repacking his suitcase off and on

throughout the week, and to catch him staring off into space at 7:30 sharp every evening.

She worried about him during the week he was in Easton, calling him faithfully at his hotel room every evening to hear about his day and to make sure he hadn't had an extended episode that had left him staring at an ugly painting on a hotel room wall all week long. The phone calls ultimately did little to ease her concerns, but they at least assured her that he was alive, breathing, and functioning for most of each day that he was away.

He had come back from the trip looking more chipper and re-laxed than he had in months, and Janie's fears subsided. He was his usual self: gregarious and affectionate with her and gruff and hard-nosed with everyone else. However, in the past few days the gawping fits had started back up. She caught him in the study not long past dinnertime on the evening after the Christian education committee meeting. Having completely forgotten the episodes, Janie burst into the study with a cup of strong coffee for him, chattering away in an attempt to keep life as normal as possible in the aftermath of the news about Emily Saunders. There was Everett, sitting slumped in his high-back leather desk chair, eyes fixed in rapt attention on his Montblanc pen in the pencil mug. She'd cut herself off in mid-sentence and near-ly spilled the coffee, but even this sudden change in Janie's behavior had gone unnoticed by the entranced Everett.

And it had continued to happen in the nights since. And here she stood in front of Everett in his study again, waving her hand in front of his face, hoping to snap him out of his reverie. To no avail.

She walked around and stood directly in front of him, bending her knees and crouching to look him in the eye as he sat hunched in the chair as usual.

"Everett?" she said tentatively, not sure she should break him out of his state too suddenly. She brought her hand up and gently touched his face, hoping the skin-to-skin contact would bring him out of it.

He flinched slightly at her touch, and slowly his face turned to meet hers.

"Everett?" she repeated, gazing into his eyes and trying to see what he was seeing.

"Yes?" he asked, unaware that he had been acting strangely.

"Where were you just now?" she asked, trying to find a way to broach the subject gracefully.

He frowned. "Where *was* I?" Janie was now sure he didn't realize he'd been doing this.

"Yes, sweetheart. I came in here and you were staring at ... nothing."

"I was?"

"Yes. It happened yesterday too."

"It did?"

She was at least glad to see this was bothering him. It would have been harder to handle if he had discounted it as her imagination or tried to justify it as something too minor to worry about.

"Yes! And lots of other nights, too. Always here in the study. Always after dinner like this."

He looked deep into her eyes, amazed at what she was saying.

"I'm beginning to think it's my cooking."

She blushed, smiling at him sweetly. His worried visage softened and he smiled too.

"No, of course not, honey." He thought for a moment. "I had no idea I was doing that. How long do I look like that?"

Janie thought for a moment. "Long enough for me to notice. To count to a hundred. To worry."

He took her hands in his. "Janie, honey, I'm so sorry. I wish you'd mentioned this before."

"I thought about it. But then it stopped for a while, so I didn't worry about it anymore. Till it started back up the other night. And now I'm really worried."

"I'm sure I'm fine, Janie. I just get distracted more easily, I guess. Part of getting older."

"No, it's not being distracted, and you know it. If you were just distracted, you would at least remember it was happening in the first place. I think you should see the doctor about it. See what he says. Maybe there's an easy answer."

"The doctor?"

"Well, yes, Everett. In case there's something medically wrong. We should rule that out first, don't you think?"

"I guess."

"Why? Do you have a different idea about how to handle this?"

He looked at her, expressionless. "I was thinking maybe I should call Ray."

"Pastor Ray? Whatever for?"

"Long story, Janie. Very long story."

She crouched closer to him, clasping his hands firmly in hers now. "I have time, Everett. I have nothing but time."

She felt his hands get suddenly clammy and start shaking in her grasp. His face cinched in pain, and she felt her heart leap into her throat with apprehension.

"Okay. There are some things you should know about me. Things I never told you. Get off the floor, honey, and let's go sit in the living room. This isn't going to be easy."

+ + + + +

THE BLOOD FLOWED FREELY FROM HIS NOSE AND MOUTH. He ran his inflamed tongue around the inside of his mouth, tasted blood, and felt a loose tooth on the lower left side. His whole head flared in pain.

"Frank, stop it!" Everett spluttered through blood and a swollen face. "C'mon, I mean it. Quit it!"

Frank continued to pummel Everett, laughing out loud and not caring who heard him. Everett knew, though, that no one heard him. They were out behind the garage, which bordered the rarely used back alley dividing their small property from the neighbors' on the next street. It was past dark but not too late at night, so no one in the house missed them yet. Frank counted on this, had calculated the situation carefully, and gave Everett another wallop in the nose. Fresh blood flew everywhere. Frank seemed unconcerned about blood hitting their clothing. Everett knew Frank was already concocting a good cover-up story for the blood on their shirts. Frank was always two or three moves ahead of his younger, foolhardy brother.

Just when Everett thought he couldn't stand another blow to his already aching head, Frank grabbed both of Everett's ears and leaned down close to his face.

"You make me sick, you little weasel. Grow a backbone, Everett, before you have to crawl to school every morning."

Frank twisted Everett's ears, and Everett let out a wail. Frank touched his nose to Everett's bloodied one, then chomped down hard and bit Everett's nose till he felt something give way. Everett immediately felt too woozy to even scream for help. He went limp under Frank's grasp and choked on the blood still in his mouth.

Frank suddenly let go of Everett's ears and sat back to look at him a little better under the street lamp in the alleyway.

"Everett? Knock it off. I'm not going to stop just because you're playing possum."

Everett lay there silently, sprawled on the ground and looking lifeless as a rag doll. Frank looked concerned.

"Everett? You okay? Quit it! You're scaring me."

Frank's insistence was to no avail. Everett was not moving. His breathing was labored, with raspy, rattly noises coming from his gaping mouth, blood trickling out one corner and onto his chin. Frank used a sleeve to mop up the worst of the dripping blood, while trying to shake Everett as gently as possible.

"I swear if you don't knock it off and snap out of it, I'll beat you to a pulp."

When this overused but usually effective tactic failed to work, Frank had had enough and realized that he'd crossed all the wrong boundaries this time.

"Mom! Dad! Come here—quick!" He dumped Everett onto the ground and ran for the back door of the house.

+ + + + +

EVERETT'S RECUPERATION WAS SWIFT, like that of most kids who are used to mistreatment at the hands of family members. He needed stitches, a few ice patches, and some close watching from Mom and Dad for a possible concussion. He was also getting the eagle-eye from Frank, who was there when Everett came out of his "episode" (what his mother was calling it now), making it plain with the mere look on his face that tattling was not allowed. Frank had piped up immediately upon Everett's awakening, launching into the explanation his parents had already heard so that Everett would hear it and know what the official story was going to be. Something about some guys they'd never seen before—not from the neighborhood, the bully types who beat up on kids smaller than they are. Et cetera, et cetera. Everett did a lot of nodding and pointing at Frank as he told the story again as his parents listened, shaking their heads in disbelief and fear for their sons once they were all back home. Everett knew how to save his own hide. This hospital was a place he didn't want to see ever again.

+ + + + +

YEARS LATER, IN HIGH SCHOOL, EVERETT GREW TALL and formidable, his chest and arms filling out and his stature an impressive six-foot-three. With a lot of focused hard work throughout high school, he did amazingly well in all of his college preparatory classes and looked forward to going away to school after graduation, as much to get away from his family as to study engineering. Frank, who had graduated several years earlier, was working full-time for Smitty, a second-rate auto mechanic who had taken care of the Newmans' cars over the years. Frank was his third-rate assistant. Smitty had needed a go-fer right around the time Frank graduated high school (although "barely passed high school" was a more accurate description), and Frank had little ambition beyond next Saturday night's drinking spree. The two were a good match.

One fine spring day, while Everett was tucked away at college in Cleveland, the decrepit hydraulic vehicle lift under which Frank routinely worked let loose in a fluke accident. Oil blew out at its connections and the lift collapsed, taking with it a green 1961 Chevy Impala brought in for an oil change, pulverizing Frank in what Everett later categorized only as a crass sense of poetic justice.

Shortly after this otherwise tragic event, Everett Newman came to believe in an almighty and loving God.

+ + + + +

AFTER GRADUATING WITH A BACHELOR'S DEGREE in electrical engineering from Fenn College in Cleveland, Everett stayed in the Cleveland area, mostly to be near his sweetheart, Jane Andrews. She was lovely, sincere, and trusted him implicitly. He was awed by her ability to trust and love; it inspired him in ways he didn't know were possible. He craved being near her, knowing she was good for him, right for him.

She also didn't pry, didn't push, didn't nag. So, when Everett needed to be alone because he felt one of his episodes coming on, she never questioned it—because she never knew. He could make up just about any story and she found it likely enough to latch onto. With his episodes coming regularly since just before Frank's death, Everett truly craved being near Janie, knowing her trusting naiveté was not good for him. He felt himself sliding further down the slippery slope of stealth. She never knew about the bloody assault for which he had been arrested. It had happened during Everett's sophomore year, before they met, and since it had never gone to court or become part of his record, he saw no need to scare her away by telling her about it.

Not until now. In the study. After thirty-two years of otherwise blissful marriage.

16

HEARING THE PHONE RING and assuming Pastor Ray was going to pick it up, Peter motioned to Ray silently as he walked into the office unannounced, pointing to the over-stuffed chair next to Ray's desk and raising his eyebrows in a question.

Ray, still looking at the ringing phone with his peripheral vision, nodded at Peter, waving him down into the chair in an overly welcoming gesture. He turned from the phone when it stopped ringing and smiled wide.

"Peter, hi! I'm going to let the voice mail get that. Been on the phone enough for one day." *One lifetime*, he thought cynically.

Peter managed a weak smile. "That bad, huh? Is anyone having a *good* day today?" he asked, flopping his tall frame into the flowery cushioned chair he'd been offered.

"The gossips sure are," Ray said bluntly, skating dangerously close to the topic already hovering between them. He leaned back in his chair, putting his feet up on the desk and clasping his hands together behind his head. "What can I do for you, Pete?" He tried to sound casual, relaxed, reassuring. Peter was looking at him like he was mildly and condescendingly nuts.

"Not quite sure, actually. I stopped by your house, but Holly said you'd be here the rest of the afternoon."

Ray unclasped his hands and brought his feet down off the desk, planting them firmly back onto the floor. His palms were sweating already, and he slowly ran his hands up and down along the thighs of his pants, trying to get rid of the clamminess. He laughed nervously and cast his gaze to the floor in front of his feet.

"Yeah, I've been here fielding phone calls for hours."

Peter grunted. "Must be a slow news day," he said, and when Ray looked up, surprised, he found Peter staring at him blankly. He didn't know what to make of this bluntness. Or just how gingerly to proceed.

"Peter ..." he began, again shifting his eyes to his feet. "Is there something you'd like to tell me?"

Ray hesitated to look up, but as the silence lengthened out into infinity, he pulled his stare away from his shoes and slowly lifted it up to meet Peter's. Still blank.

"Probably nothing to tell you that you haven't heard on the phone today a million times already."

Hard to read that tone, Ray thought. Guilt? Sarcasm? Anger? Bitterness? Or just confusion?

"So, you know."

Now Peter's gaze fell to the floor. "About Emily? Yeah, I know. Found out last night, as a matter of fact."

"Did Emily call you?"

Peter shook his head. "No, I haven't heard from her at all yet. I tried calling her earlier but her line was busy. I may stop over there on my way home from here."

"Good thinking," Ray offered. "My guess is, she could use a friend right about now." He sighed. "May I ask how you found out, Peter? I know you're not on the C.E. committee, so you weren't at the meeting last night."

"No, you're right, I wasn't. But I got a call from Everett not long after the meeting was over."

Ray looked up briskly, to find Peter already staring at him. "Everett? Everett Newman? Why the devil would he call you about this?"

"Oh, I could hear it in his voice. He couldn't wait to tell me. He was almost giddy when he realized I hadn't heard the news yet." Peter scowled and gripped the armrests of the chair tightly, his knuckles white and muscles taut. "I'll never understand that man."

Ray relaxed slightly and leaned back in the desk chair. "He's not that hard to understand, really. He's a sinner, just like you and me. Only his sins are usually right out there for all of us to see. In Everett's case, you see the sins and he hides the good deeds. The opposite of most people, really. Most of us hide our sins and try to flaunt our good deeds."

Peter frowned at this odd and very forgiving assessment of Everett Newman. Ray continued.

"It's really a refreshing way to look at someone. And frankly, I'd rather know what sins I'm dealing with in a person than have to dig deep to find them before I can help the person deal with them."

Peter frowned more. It still wasn't adding up.

"No, really. I mean it. Sure, he's annoying as can be at times like this—let's face it, the man has no tact whatsoever—but at least you always know what you're dealing with in Everett."

Peter continued his silence.

"Right?" Ray offered, smiling what he hoped was an encouraging smile for Peter.

"I see your point, Ray."

"Good."

"But still, the man called me to gloat. To gloat, Ray! It was ugly."

Ray's thoughts wandered away from Emily and Peter and landed squarely on a now-ancient counseling session with Everett Newman.

✦ ✦ ✦ ✦ ✦

"Pastor, I have this problem with anger."

"A lot of people do, Everett. Tell me more."

"Well, Pastor, before I lived here, I was out in Cleveland, as you

know. You didn't know me then, but I was a nasty sonofabitch. Oh, sorry,
Pastor. Didn't mean to curse like that, but really, it's the only word to
describe me."

    "No problem. Go on, Everett. Tell me about your anger."

    "Pastor, when I was younger, I was arrested for assault. Now, it never
went to court—long story on that one—but I beat a man senseless one
night."

    "Were you drinking, Everett?"

    "No, Pastor, I don't touch the stuff. Never have. I was just ... angry."

    "What did he do to you to make you angry?"

    "Nothing, really. I was just ... mad."

    "I see."

✝ ✝ ✝ ✝ ✝

RAY SHOOK HIMSELF OUT OF HIS REVERIE. "Well, Peter, this really
shouldn't be about Everett anyway. I'll have a talk with him at some
point, too. For now, though, how are you handling the news?"

    Peter sighed loudly. "How should I handle it? It's probably better
I haven't spoken to Emily yet. Who knows what I would have said to
her? Probably something stupid that'd just make her cry."

    Ray shook his head. "I dunno about that, Pete. Emily's a stronger
woman than perhaps you or I give her credit for. She hasn't come running to me yet. So far she's handling it on her own."

    "No, that's not it. She'd stay away from you on purpose. She'd be
ashamed, embarrassed, whatever. The last thing she'd want is to turn
this into a three-ring circus for everyone. Like when Jonathan died."

    "I thought the church rallied around her swimmingly when that
happened," Ray added naively.

    "To a point. The meals were great. She needed that kind of help.
But the rest—it was a nightmare for her. She hated being talked about
and stared at."

    Ray blinked.

    "And now it's going to happen all over again, only maybe without the meals. Of course she wouldn't call you. She'd stay home and hide. Which is probably why I haven't heard from her either."

"I can honestly say I hadn't thought of it that way, Peter. Do you think she'd find a visit or a call from me intrusive right now?"

Peter shook his head. "I don't know."

"What about a visit from Holly instead?"

"I'd have to talk to her myself first and find out. I know she really likes Holly."

Ray shifted in his chair, the metal bracings on the back rest groaning as he moved. "Pete, how much do you really know about what's happened to Emily in the past couple of months?" He let the question hang in midair, watching Peter absorb it and think about it briefly before speaking.

"You mean, what do I know about the attack? That kind of thing?"

Ray nodded uncertainly. He didn't want to lead Peter in any given direction, but rather wanted him to find his own way to tell his side of the story.

"Well, she left Faith and Mikey with me for the weekend for her class reunion—you already knew that. She'd call and check in during the mornings rather than at night, so she could talk to the kids. She said there were always reunion things going on in the evenings and she was busy. She was a little fuzzy on exactly when she'd be getting back and since I was on a layoff for Thanksgiving, I didn't mind having the kids an extra day or so.

"When I didn't hear from her for a day or two after the reunion, the kids started to get upset and I got worried. The hotel said no, she hadn't checked out and was still listed as a guest. I hoped she'd just found a bunch of friends to hang out with, and they'd all decided to stay a few extra days to relive old times or something."

He shrugged and relaxed his grip on the chair's overstuffed armrests. A wavy lock of sandy hair fell in his face, and he tossed his head to put it back where it belonged.

"Just when I was getting really nervous about it, I got a call from a nurse at the hospital where they'd taken her after they found her by the river. By then she was awake again and had asked the nurse to call me. The nurse gave me the basic rundown on what had happened: the attack, Emily's injuries, how lucky she was that someone found her, all that stuff. A little later Emily called me herself."

Peter stopped, tapping his foot nervously on the floor. Ray wasn't sure whether to inject some pastoral advice at this point, or to wait for Peter to continue his story. When Peter continued to tap his foot and didn't continue talking, Ray knew he had to cover the growing silence.

"Peter, did the nurse mention to you anything about Emily being ... assaulted?" Was there a delicate way to put this? Did it matter at this point?

"Well, that's how she got the injuries, Ray. I'm not sure I get what you mean."

Ray bore his gaze into Peter a little more harshly, and when Peter looked up to see that gaze, it was obvious that something had finally clicked.

"Oh, you mean ... *assaulted.*" Neither one of them could say it. Ray wondered what that said about the two of them, but shrugged it off as tertiary to the discussion at hand.

"Yes, assaulted. That's what everyone's saying to me on the phone today." Ray took a deep breath and decided to dive into the middle of the proverbial pool. "Unless you have a better explanation for how this happened."

Peter met Ray's frown squarely with his own and didn't blink. "No. Why would I?"

Ray couldn't read Peter well enough to determine if Peter was asking him honestly or accusing him. He made a mental note to get to know his church members a little better in the future. More pastoral visits with the members. Yes, that was a good idea.

"No reason, really. I just never heard anything when Emily first came back that would have indicated she had been ... you know." Ray coughed uncomfortably.

"Raped?" Peter offered, still frowning at Ray.

"Yes, raped," Ray finally breathed out with a sigh. "Raped."

There. It was out there. It had been said. Had Emily been raped during the attack?

"I thought of that, but then I remembered that Emily was unconscious because that bastard hit her on the head and knocked her out."

Ray winced imperceptibly.

"Sorry, Ray. Didn't mean to put it like that."

"'S'okay. Perfectly understandable, given the circumstances."

"She wouldn't have remembered anything anyway."

"Wouldn't the hospital staff have said something to her about it after she woke up, though?" Ray asked.

Peter shrugged. "I don't know. I don't know how they do those things. And I certainly don't know how they do them in Easton."

Ray suddenly stood from his chair, straightening to his full height and stretching a little. "Well, sounds to me like the only way around this awkwardness is for someone to talk directly to Emily. I'm not inclined to let the rumor mill keep grinding when there's a way to stop it dead. I think I'll talk to Holly about this and see which of us she thinks ought to pay Emily a visit."

Taking his cue from Ray, Peter stood and slipped his hand into his front jeans pocket for his truck keys. "You don't want me to go talk to her first?"

"No, unless you really want to head over there now. It'll be a little while till Holly or I get over there. I just don't want her to feel ganged-up on."

"I don't know what I'm going to do." Peter turned away from Ray, toward the door, and ran his free hand through his hair in a nervous gesture of frustration. "I'll decide once I'm on the road."

"Fair enough," Ray conceded. "You do what you have to. We'll get this straightened out and find out what's best for everyone soon enough."

Without acknowledging Ray's last comment, Peter opened the office door and strode back into the parking lot toward his truck. Ray stood in the office watching him leave, hands crossed tightly across his chest, biting his lip till he felt a sharp sting and tasted his own blood.

"Sonofabitch," he said softly, immediately catching himself and mumbling a quick confession, and then fumbled for his own keys so he could lock up the office and get home to Holly.

17

I WAS GETTING TIRED OF WAKING UP FROM A NAP feeling like I never slept. I always sat up and instantly felt like someone had socked me in the gut with a massive boxing glove. It was impossible to tell if I felt this way because I was pregnant or because everyone knew I was pregnant. Not that it much mattered—feeling like crap had the same effect on me no matter how it happened.

So, I sat up in bed for a while, trying to adjust my equilibrium to reality, rubbing my stinging eyes, stretching till I nearly lost my sit-up balance and fell back onto the bed. Every afternoon when I tried to nap it was this same routine, and it never really helped. I still felt queasy, uneasy, and totally *not* ready for the world.

Today I was on the bed, pretending I was reading a good book when, really, I was sitting there running worst-case scenarios of the rest of my pathetic life. None of them made me feel any better, but I didn't know why I expected anything different, since this was usually part of the definition of a worst-case scenario. I guess what made me feel so bad about this musing was that I could come up with *so many* bad possibilities—and they were all worse than what was actually happening. It was no comfort to realize that things could still get so much worse. What started as an exercise in trying to think, "Cheer up, things could be worse," had turned into a list of ways in which things could spiral further downward, uncontrolled and unstoppable. Things still could get worse. Far worse.

Life as a pessimist really sucked.

Feeling guilty for languishing, I climbed off the bed and grabbed my robe off the foot of the bed. I was still in my sleeping T-shirt and a ratty pair of flannel drawstring pants. My fuzzy slippers were at opposite ends of the bedroom, having been kicked off hastily late last night when I came up to bed. I walked to the left one, shimmied my foot into it, and shuffled to the right one by the door so I could smoosh my foot into that one before heading down the steps. Glancing at the clock radio, I saw it flip over to 3:00 p.m. *Good grief, why do I need so many naps?* I didn't remember being this lethargic during the other two pregnancies. Then again, I hadn't been fodder for the ol' church gossip column during the last two pregnancies, either.

I decided to stop dialing Ray Compton's office number from the upstairs phone—bad karma or something, I thought, and almost chuckled to myself. Maybe there was a reason I wasn't getting through to him today. Maybe I shouldn't be talking to my pastor about this just yet. But most of me wanted desperately to talk to someone, and who better than your pastor at a time like this?

Well, okay, Peter, for one. My fingers, though, just weren't in the mood to dial his number today. He'd probably already heard the news, and the fact that he hadn't called or stopped by yet told me more than I wanted to know about what he was thinking. I may have been holding our relationship at arm's length as best I could, but right now I still felt a sense of loss. Maybe it was losing the relationship itself, or just the control over it.

My slippered feet hit the bottom step and I turned toward the kitchen. Hot cocoa, anyone?

In an ongoing effort to do mundane things that felt familiar and also to ward off the inevitable clash with the outside world, I lumbered into the kitchen and grabbed the kettle off the back burner.

Dumping out the old water from a few days ago, I rinsed the pot out and filled it with fresh water before setting it back onto the burner and turning it on high. The soft whoosh of the burner lighting was another small familiar thing that felt right. As the gas did its work starting to heat the water, I reached into the cupboard to the right of the stove and found the canister of powdered hot chocolate mix. I grabbed my favorite mug (a warped thing that looked as if someone crushed it, with "I Got SMASHED in Vegas!" festooned across the front) and a spoon to scoop out the five heaping spoonfuls. The side of the canister called for four, but this felt like a five-spoonful day to me. Plus whipped cream. Lots of whipped cream. Definitely.

I was stirring the hot water into the mug of powder, making sure none of it caked onto the bottom of the mug in a gross clump, when the doorbell rang. I secretly hoped it wasn't Cassie bringing the kids back. She knew I was really home today, playing hooky from work, but still ... I just wasn't up for mommyhood at all once Meg had left after having pizza. Not now that I was pregnant. I ran that perversely ironic thought through my head again and almost laughed. Almost.

Leaving the hot chocolate to cool on the countertop, I closed my robe more snugly over the T-shirt and flannel pants and scuffled to the front door. I wished for one of those peepholes in the door as I braced myself for whatever awaited me on the other side. Maybe the Publishers Clearing House gang was out there with balloons and a ridiculously big cardboard check. Hand firmly gripping the smooth brass doorknob, I twisted it suddenly and jerked the door open. I fought the urge to screw my eyes shut tight against the face opposite me—and there stood Peter Bellows, hands in his front jeans pockets, locks of hair blowing across his forehead, out of place and scruffy, not typical of him. He alternated between looking me in the eye and casting his gaze down at the straw mat under his feet. Neither one of us looked as if we got much sleep last night.

"Peter," I said simply.

"Emily," he returned.

Amenities out of the way, I stepped aside to wave him in past me. He stood on the porch for a few more seconds, hands still deep in his pockets. I couldn't read his face. Embarrassment? Awkwardness? Fear? Dread? Did he want an engraved invitation, or what?

"Peter, come in," I said finally, stating the obvious for someone whose mind didn't seem to be on social graces right now. His face cleared of its muddled cloud and he straightened to his full height, his hands coming out of his pockets.

He edged past me and into the house, taking particular care not to brush up against me in any way, a precaution he wouldn't have taken yesterday. Although I didn't think he meant for me to notice this slight, I did. And I was unsure how to process the information. Was he being gracious for my benefit or cautious for his own?

I've got to stop second-guessing everything and everyone.

The door closed behind us when I shoved it with my fuzzy foot. It was a tad louder than I would have liked, and in reaction Peter spun around to face me. There was that awkward staring contest again.

"Peter ..." I began hastily.

"Emily ..." he began at the same time.

We chuckled uncomfortably at each other, which created its own awkwardness. This was quickly becoming, well, awkward.

I shook my head and hands at him. "Peter, no, let me speak."

He nodded silently, acquiescing.

"Peter," I began again. "I'm so sorry I didn't tell you sooner. To be honest, I was still getting used to the whole idea." I sighed, hoping he'd go easy on me. "I'm not handling any of this very well. I mean, look at me," I said, tugging at my bathrobe as if to show it off. "It's the middle of the afternoon and I'm back in my jammies."

Peter nodded some more and walked over to me, his arms outstretched. "It's all right," he said, and I was suddenly grateful for his warm, overly platonic hug. "I hope I haven't been the cause of any of your worrying."

I gently broke free of him. "No, no, of course not. You? Never." It was obvious that he believed me, but whether or not *I* believed me is a different story. I had taken to fibbing like I was some kind of freakish X-chromosome Pinocchio.

Turning away from him, I walked back to the kitchen and my cocoa. I heard him behind me and asked without turning, "I put water on to boil. You want some hot cocoa?"

"Yeah, you know, that sounds great. Can I get it myself?" he offered.

"No, that's all right. I don't mind." I reached back into the cupboard for another mug (a pink one with "World's Best Mom!" in ridiculously large, cartoony block letters). I spooned the heaps of powder into the mug and added the still-hot water from the tea kettle, stirring it into a creamy liquid with the same spoon. I didn't think he'd mind me using the same spoon. Last I heard, pregnancy wasn't contagious.

He reached for the mug before I could hand it to him, and our fingers touched lightly as we passed the cocoa from maker to drinker. A small burst of adrenaline zipped through me before I could quell it properly, and I felt suitably stupid. Once he had the mug in his own hand, I pulled mine back, wondering what I would say next to keep the situation from becoming unbearably slow and tense. Every word I'd spoken so far—which hadn't been much, granted—had been pulled from inside me with a pair of tiny tweezers, and it was going to get excruciating all too soon.

Peter automatically turned and walked back into the living room to get more comfortable, and I followed, with my twisted Vegas mug warming up my hands. He sat on the couch, leaving me either the rocking chair or the old recliner opposite him. I opted for my grandmother's old oak rocking chair, which gave me something to do to work off the nervous energy while we talked. The mock-bent mug didn't fit properly onto the cork coaster on the end table and I gave up and held it with both hands in my lap instead. This forced me to rock more slowly than I would have liked, and I realized the adrenaline buzz would be tough to work off while rocking this gently in the chair.

"Peter," I sighed, not wanting to dive into this whole mess but knowing it had become a lot like death, childbirth, and taxes: inevitable once you hit a certain age and got yourself into a compromising situation. I took a big gulp of the too-hot cocoa and gasped a little as it scorched its way down my throat. But, at least now I could rock the chair a little more forcefully without making a brown, hot puddle in my lap.

"I didn't mean to *not* call you last night. I didn't even mean for everyone to find out last night. I only found out myself a little while ago. And it's been a nightmare ever since. It's all I've been thinking about. It just kinda ... came out last night at the meeting. I didn't want everyone to find out like that."

He nodded, sipping his cocoa a lot more carefully than I'd been doing. "I figured as much. But when you didn't call me, I wasn't sure whether to come over here or not. I tried calling a few times but kept getting a busy signal."

"I was probably either calling Ray or I had the phone off the hook. I didn't want to risk calls from ... certain people."

"Like Everett Newman?" Peter spit out, sounding quite disgusted.

"Well, him, yeah, and a few of the women. The ones who talked last time. When Jonathan died."

"I don't think the women are the ones to worry about. They were probably just trying to figure out how to help you. But Everett ... he's a different story. I just don't trust that man." Peter was frowning hard now, visibly angry at something. He was clutching the mug tightly in both hands, and I half expected the "World's Best Mom!" mug to end up looking like the Vegas mug if he didn't loosen his grip on it soon.

"I dislike Everett as much as the next person—well, probably more. But you look like you're ready to jump down the guy's throat. I'm not sure I want to know what happened between you two," I said, meaning exactly the opposite of what I just said.

"He's the reason I found out what happened at the meeting last night."

I was confused by this. "Meaning what, exactly?"

"Meaning," Peter replied, moving forward on the couch until he was sitting on the very edge of the seat, "he called me to tell me about

it. Probably the second he got home, judging from when he called
me."

I stopped rocking and put the mug down on the end table, missing the coaster entirely and putting it on the bare wood. "Everett
called you—specifically to tell you that? Did he have some other reason to call?" I asked, hoping against hope.

"No, no other reason. Just to gloat—about what had happened to
you and the fact that I didn't know about it yet."

I looked down at my hands in my lap and saw that they were
shaking. "The bastard," I said.

"The bastard," Peter echoed. I was stunned, as much by Peter's
swearing as by Everett's utter lack of tact and decorum. Not that I
would ever accuse Everett Newman of tact in any situation, least of all
one involving getting me into trouble with my church beau. Everett
was in his element.

"He frightens me," I blurted out, not realizing how deeply I believed this until I heard myself say it in a rare unguarded moment.

Peter looked up at me in a jolt. "Why would you say that?" He
was suddenly very curious about why I felt this way.

"Doesn't he creep you out too?" I asked, seeking confirmation of
my sheepishness.

"Frankly, on a bad day I think he creeps out *God*."

I laughed out loud and the smile stayed on my face. Peter looked
me squarely in the eye and seemed relieved to see me smiling.

It felt good to be smiling, but it seemed a long way from relief. A
long way.

18

PETER AND I SAT AND TALKED ABOUT EVERETT a while longer. To me, discussing Everett—although entirely distasteful— was preferable to discussing my pregnancy or the imaginary church paparazzi swirling around me in my mind. Badmouthing Everett had a comfort-zone quality about it, probably because so many of us engaged in the activity so often. The man was nitpicked by his peers more than a baboon in the zoo with a bad case of lice. He brought it on himself, to be blunt, because he had no tact and seemed to revel in the misfortunes of those he considered his political or theological inferiors. And, in Everett's mind, that meant just about everyone except his wife, Janie. And Pastor Ray. Everett respected authority figures in an almost unnatural way, especially ecclesiastical authorities. He could quote Deuteronomy 25:4—about not muzzling the ox while it treaded out the grain—in five different Bible translations.

And he even knew what the verse meant, too. Usually I had to hear that one a few times in my head before I made sense of it all over again. Often, understanding Old Testament quotes properly made me feel like I was back in junior high German class translating snippets of sentences for Herr Ascherbauer, a phrase here or there making some sense but the whole sentence holding together in my head only by a thin thread of logic and grammar I held in my proverbially clenched teeth.

I was dismayed to hear from Peter that the whole congregation had been bombarding Ray with calls that day. Peter took it as a sign that people didn't have anything better to do and that it was probably a good sign for the congregation's level of sanctification if the most scandalous thing happening in our ranks was me getting beat up and "assaulted." Peter said the word "assaulted" so delicately and haltingly that I knew he'd meant to say "raped" but couldn't bring himself to do it in my presence.

Meanwhile, I sat there feeling incredibly foolish that: (a) Peter had enough faith in me to be certain that the only explanation for this situation was me having been "assaulted"; and (b) Peter was such a naive, sheltered, glass-is-half-full kind of guy that he saw the gossiping about this as a good sign.

I wasn't sure if I suddenly felt very worldly-wise and savvy or just plain slutty. Either way, I felt very much out of Peter's league in all sorts of bad ways.

"Ray's probably on his way over here," Peter blurted out at one point, as he gulped down the last swallow of his tepid cocoa and plunked the mug dead-center onto the cork coaster on the coffee table.

I clutched my own mug a little tighter at that pronouncement. "Here? Now?" I tried not to sound as unnerved by that as I was. A girl could easily feel ganged-up-on around here if things continued in this direction.

Peter nodded, catching a drop of sticky cocoa on the corner of his mouth with his thumb and unceremoniously wiping it onto the thigh of his jeans, not even wondering if I'd seen it. I had. But he'd done it with such finesse and gracefulness that I actually admired it.

Peter had already told me about the events leading up to his showing up on my doorstep earlier. "Why would Ray need to come over here today if he sent you over first?"

"Well, he didn't really send me over ... not officially. He just said I could come over here first to talk to you if I felt I had to ... before he came over later."

I stood and circled the rocking chair once with the mug in my hand. "I wish he would have thought to send over Holly instead."

"Oh, I forgot—it could be Holly coming. One of them is probably coming over but I don't know which one. He didn't know either."

I stopped circling the chair like my own vulture and looked at Peter. "Now I'm totally confused. Which one of them is coming over?"

"I dunno. He hadn't decided yet by the time I left. He wanted to go home and talk to Holly first and then decide."

"Oh. Great. Another kaffeeklatsch about me."

"I didn't really think of it that way. They keep things confidential between them—as the pastor and the pastor's wife."

I blinked. "Except when they're talking to you, apparently."

Okay, that was a little too snide for my own good, but I felt it bubbling to the surface again. All of it. It was like I couldn't separate the pieces of a succession of bad events anymore. Once one of them made its way to the front burner, the whole stove lit up and all four mental burners flared up, out of control. It was my husband's car accident all over again, the same panic, the same fear, the same growing, gnawing realization that life had shifted under me, making me lose my balance, and that everyone around me was watching me plummet. Again. It felt utterly devastating, and yet entirely too familiar. Once I started thinking about that day, it happened all over again, fresh as dew, and twice as clammy.

+ + + + +

"Mommy—phone!"

I had come into the kitchen that day from the back porch, carrying baby Mikey on my hip, and I took the phone from Faith, who was far too young to be answering it for me—not that this stopped her.

"Hello, Saunders."

"Mrs. Saunders?"

"Yes, this is Mrs. Saunders. Who is this?"

"Mrs. Jonathan Saunders?"

Mikey was wriggling to get down so he could army-crawl across the floor and eat Fweepit's cat food out of the bowl, and I was getting a little impatient with the woman on the phone.

"Yes, this is Mrs. Jonathan Saunders. Can I help you?" I asked, more than a little perturbed at the interruption.

"Mrs. Saunders, this is Nurse O'Rourke down at West Side General Hospital." I felt my stomach flip-flop at the word "hospital."

"Yes?" I asked warily.

"I'm sorry to tell you this over the phone, but your husband's been in an accident."

I let Mikey slip off my hip and noiselessly onto the floor, and I let the receiver plummet to the linoleum and clunk and bounce once before I picked it up again.

"Accident?" Surely she was mistaken.

"Yes, ma'am. I believe a pickup truck ran a red light and hit his car broadside. Right now he's in surgery."

"Is ... is he going to be all right?" I asked, watching with no emotion as Mikey stuffed fistfuls of Little Friskies into his mouth.

"I can't say for sure, Mrs. Saunders. I suggest you get down here as soon as you can, though." She hesitated, and then uttered three words that would stick in my craw for years: "Just in case."

Faith was tugging at my jeans and pointing at Mikey, whose face was rapidly turning a pasty barn-red from the half-crunched, half-spit-out cat food he had smeared all over it. I heard Ernie singing from the living room TV about his rubber duckie. I faintly heard Nurse O'Rourke telling me something else, but I didn't hear what she said because I was slowly hanging the receiver back onto the phone on the wall.

I picked the receiver right back up again and dialed Meg's number without thinking. It rang three times before Meg answered, and I spent that time watching Faith try to scrape the glop of cat food off Mikey's face with a napkin. She was grimacing as a little mommy might, with a look that communicated personal offense as well as disapproval. Mikey was snapping his head from side to side, deftly keeping his artwork away from her.

"Hello?" Meg answered.

"Meg, this is Emily."

"Hi. What's up?"

"I just got a call from some stupid prick from West Side General."

"Emily!" Meg gasped. "What's the matter. Are you all right?"

"No."

"What happened?" she asked hastily.

"It's Jon. He's been in a car accident."

"Oh my God," she said. I had never heard her take the Lord's name in vain. "Is he all right?"

I didn't say anything. I froze up. Life around my feet was kiddie chaos, and my jaws locked.

"I'm coming right over. Stay there," Meg commanded, and she hung up the phone.

I don't know how long it took her to fight the zillion traffic lights between our houses. But when she arrived and came flying in the front door and through the dining room into the kitchen, I was sitting on the floor still clutching the receiver, and Mikey and Faith were spilling off my lap, both of them looking at their dazed mother and crying.

Meg took the receiver out of my hand and hung it back up. She lifted the kids off my lap, carried Mikey over to the sink to wipe off his face, and told Faith that I would be fine, that she should go in and watch the end of *Sesame Street*. I watched Meg do all my duties with this distracted kind of fascination, admiring her cool adroitness and thanking God that I didn't have to chisel the dried cat food off Mikey's face.

She put Mikey in the playpen in the dining room, and came back to help me stand up. "Emily, we're going to drop the kids off at Cassie's house, and I'm going to drive you to West Side General." I nodded, and we headed off step by step, efficiently and methodically, to the predestined downfall of the Saunders household.

In Meg's Volkswagen, after the kids were dumped off hurriedly at Cassie's, I kept hearing this old joke run through my head:

What did the Calvinist say when he fell down the stairs?

"Whew—I'm glad that's over with!"

In the right context, it's one of the funniest jokes I've ever heard, the rare kind that can make me laugh again and again when I think about it just right. This time I just felt nauseous.

I think Meg talked to me off and on during the short trip to West Side General, but I can't say for sure. I was too busy tumbling around inside my own head, wishing I hadn't exposed myself in my youth to every sick horror flick in Hollywood back while Marty and I worked at the State Theater. Jonathan suddenly materialized in front of me, first as a walking zombie, then a slimy space alien, then a larger-than-life army hero on an olive green stretcher, legs half blown off and filled with shrapnel.

"Please don't let him die, please don't let him die, please don't let him die," I chanted repeatedly. I saw in my peripheral vision Meg looking at me, worried and afraid. "Please don't let him die, please don't let him die."

"Emily, do you want me to pray while we're driving?"

"Please don't let him die, please don't let him die ..."

"Okay, I'll pray," Meg answered herself. I could hear her fine now, but I couldn't bear to part with my mantra, to which I was now clinging in a pitiful attempt to ward off the inevitable.

I pitched the chorus a bit higher, but never lost the critical rhythm. "Please don't let him die, please don't let him die ..."

"Father God," Meg began at the next red light, and I heard a distinct sobbing in her voice. I was powerless to help her, or Jonathan, or me. "Please, Jesus," she begged with me, "please don't let him die."

19

A S I LISTENED TO PETER TALK about his side of what had happened since the C.E. meeting fiasco, I knew he subscribed to only one theory of how I got pregnant: the mugger-turned-rapist theory. I knew it wasn't a totally ridiculous theory, and I had moments myself where I wondered if it weren't true. And in some sick, twisted way, I sometimes wished it were true. After all, I didn't remember much of anything about the attack anyway, and was less likely to remember anything as each day passed. And, it would certainly solve more problems than it created. I could even end up a kind of tragic, noble heroine if it were true. Wait, wait. That would mean increasingly more attention, and a lifetime of stories about me, turning into larger-than-life legends told around fireplaces during free time late at night at church retreats. Maybe I should rethink this whole martyr idea. The last thing I needed or wanted was more attention. I'd had plenty for one lifetime.

Peter was delving deeper into his opinions about Everett Newman while I mused silently about my own martyrdom. I wasn't really paying attention to him, too wrapped up in my own thoughts, until I heard him say:

"I swear that man has enough hatred in his system to commit some serious crimes."

He was shaking his head, fiddling with his cocoa mug, one leg crossed on the other knee. He was listening to himself talk, not noticing that I was in another world.

"Who? Everett?"

Peter nodded.

"Really? You think so? Crimes? You mean, like, real crimes?"

"Think about it for a second," he said, uncrossing his legs and leaning forward onto the edge of the couch cushion. "It fits so well. He threatens. He intimidates. He gets in your face. Sometimes he's the most un-Christian Christian I know."

I furrowed my brow and *tsk-tsked* quietly. "Peter, I despise Everett as much as the next God-fearing person, but I just don't see him freaking out on anyone. I mean, beyond his usual yelling and screaming to get his way."

"So you don't think he could dislike someone enough to do them harm? Not even, say, you?" He raised an eyebrow at me and crossed his arms across his chest.

"Me? When did I become his arch nemesis?" I said sarcastically.

"Well, you're his current one, anyway. You're always messing up his plans for the education committee in the church budget. You bring up things he'd rather not discuss. You question things he says that he's assuming everyone already agrees with."

"But I don't do that on purpose. I just blurt things out without thinking. That doesn't seem like it would be crime-worthy, even to Everett."

"Not to you, maybe. But Everett lives for this church. It's all he has."

"In a way it's all I have, too. I was thinking the other day that pretty much all my local friends are from Calvin Pres."

"No, not like Everett. You're talking about your relationships and friendships all being tied up in the church. I'm talking about Everett's theology, beliefs, and reason for living. Plus you have a level of self-restraint that I just don't see in Everett."

I snorted. "Self-restraint? That's a nice way to put it. It's not self-restraint, Peter. It's self-loathing. I'm too embarrassed by myself to be as arrogant as Peter. Besides, I'd bet people who are as verbally arrogant as Everett don't act on their own intimidation tactics. I think they're all hot air, if you ask me. He intimidates me, sure, but deep down, Everett is as harmless as a kitten."

As if on cue, old Fweepit brushed up against my leg and purred. I reached down to rub my hand along his back, and he arched up against my hand.

Before Peter had a chance to debate me further, the doorbell rang. Again. We both looked toward the door, as if it would answer itself. Then, sensing that this was my responsibility since my name was on the mailbox outside, I stood and crossed to the front door, Fweepit at my heels.

The open door revealed Pastor Ray Compton. He was grinning almost cartoonishly, straight white teeth showing. Fweepit blinked at the incoming sunlight, too much an indoor cat to be tempted to dash out the door any longer. He didn't like the icky feeling of grass under his delicate paws. He turned and padded back into the living room, as if leading the way for Ray and me.

"Ray!" I said, trying to sound upbeat and happy to see him. Inside, though, I kept wondering how the decision had been made to send him here instead of Holly. Seeing Ray at the door instead of Holly ratcheted up the tension just a wee bit.

He offered me his hand and I shook it in a mostly perfunctory fashion, waving him inside with my other hand.

"Come in, come in," I insisted. "Peter is here."

Ray stepped in and locked eyes with Peter, who was standing in front of the couch. Ray kept grinning and now Peter was smiling too.

"Ray!" he echoed. "Glad to see you could make it."

Ray turned toward me back by the door. "I take it Peter told you I might be stopping over then. I apologize if my timing isn't good or if you're feeling a little overwhelmed today."

"Yes, he mentioned it, although he thought perhaps Holly might be coming over instead of you."

Ray frowned briefly. "Well, she and I talked about it, and I just thought it would be better if I came over. I wanted to keep this on a pastoral level for today. Nothing wrong with talking to Holly, but I wanted to make sure all the bases were covered first."

He was fumbling over his words more than was his custom, sounding almost as if he'd never counseled someone before. I wasn't sure if it was because Peter was in the room and we were all standing around somewhat formally, or because this was as weird and unique a situation for him as I felt it was. Perhaps I wasn't alone in my level of discomfort.

I pointed out the other end of the couch for Ray to occupy, and he sat. Peter followed suit, and they both looked at me.

"Ray, can I get you some hot cocoa?"

"No, Emily, I'm fine. Let's just talk a few things through, shall we?" He motioned to the rocking chair for me. I sidestepped over to the rocker and sat.

"What should we talk about first?" I asked. So many topics, and yet really, just the one.

Ray leaned forward to the front of the couch, his elbows resting on his knees in a take-charge fashion. Probably a well-rehearsed, taught-in-seminary, take-charge fashion.

"Emily, first off, let me apologize for what happened last night. All I can make of everyone's behavior is that none of them are used to this level of ... well, scandal, for lack of a better word."

I winced at the word "scandal." It was just as I feared. "Ray, you don't need to apologize for everyone else. I know how church people are, and believe me, I understand it. I don't blame anyone ... not really. If everyone's behaving themselves and not getting into any trouble, then by default I end up being the hot topic of conversation. They're only human."

Ray sighed. "Yes, they are only human. That's true."

Peter cleared his throat loudly and piped up from the other end of the couch. "It's really not fair, Ray, to ask Emily to shoulder the added burden of graciously accepting everyone's behavior after everything else she's been through. Don't add on the stress of asking her to absolve everyone else in the congregation."

"I understand, Peter, and you're absolutely right. I'm not really asking her to forgive and forget here. That's not fair to Emily, as you said." Suddenly I was being talked about in the third person by these two men, as if I weren't there at all, as if we weren't all sitting in *my* living room in *my* house.

Ray continued. "But I'm a firm believer in understanding the other point of view. It goes a long way in helping to build bridges instead of tearing them down."

I began rocking nervously in the chair, until I accidentally rocked over Fweepit's tail, sending him yowling and running for the kitchen. For a few minutes I seemed to forget what they both thought about the situation and how things had happened, and then I'd remember all over again that their take on reality was quite different from mine. And the guilt washed over me all over again. It seemed I was doomed to live with this feeling forever, like some sort of wayward Sisyphus.

"Could you guys not talk about me like I'm not even here? Besides, it's a little scary to sit here listening to two men sound like they're trying to decide what I'm going to have to do next, as if I have no say in things."

Both Ray and Peter turned away from their head-to-head discussion and toward me. They both blinked, in unison, as if they had planned it. Their blank stares made me wonder if I'd accidentally spoken in Swahili or something.

"Hello?"

"Emily, so sorry," Ray spoke up. "I didn't mean for it to sound like we were making your decisions for you."

No, of course not. Men never think like that about women.

I was amazed at how snide my thoughts became when I felt threatened or cornered. Probably one of those psychobabble "defense mechanisms."

"Sweetheart," Peter cooed, "we're just trying to help you figure out the best course of action from this point on. I don't want to see you get hurt any more than you already have."

The offer of protection was appreciated, albeit misguided in my case. I needed to get these boys off their collision course with the truth. The more they enacted mental legislation based on their version of what happened to me, the more uncomfortable I became.

"I'm fine, Peter. What I really want is to just get back on with my life and figure out how I'm going to live with this situation day to day. Beyond that, I just want to be left alone and not talked about. I don't see that happening unless I quietly pick up where I left off and go forward. Period."

I crossed my arms and stopped rocking, deciding to stare at the floor rather than make eye contact with the two men across the room from me. Fweepit had abandoned me and was nowhere in sight.

Ray spoke. "There's a lot of wisdom in that, Emily. And it's just plain practical, too. I don't see how anyone could fault you for wanting that. Not after all you've been through."

I felt like screaming, or crying. If these two used the phrase "not after all you've been through," or any variation thereof, one more time, I truly was going to let out a yell. That'd give them something to talk about for a while.

In a tense fit of frustration and internal squabbling with myself, I suddenly stood from the rocking chair, arms still crossed, and nervously tapped one foot on the floor. A brisk walk across the room, past the couch and into the kitchen, brought me into safer territory—with warm, comforting drinks and food at my fingertips. I moved the tea kettle to a different burner on the stove and turned the flame under it on high. One more try.

"Hot cocoa anyone?" I called into the living room, drumming my jittery fingers on the countertop.

Could this little get-together possibly get any more awkward?

Just as that thought blipped into one side of my head and dribbled out the other, the doorbell rang.

Again.

20

THIS ISN'T HAPPENING WAS ALL I COULD THINK as I stood staring at the new arrival on my front porch. A taxicab waited a moment longer at the curb and then, satisfied its passenger was in a safe harbor, pulled away and headed down to the intersection with the main road. I looked from the cab to the mousy-haired, gray-eyed man smiling at me sheepishly from the porch, a mere three feet from my nose. He had a large backpack slung over his right shoulder. With no better reaction in my brain, I sighed.

"Hi, Emily."

"Marty. It's you."

The smiling continued, but not by me. "Yup. Me. Here on your porch. How are you?"

"I didn't realize you were coming."

"I figured I had to come, even just for a short visit. Seemed like the right thing to do."

"Calling first would have been the right thing to do," I countered, casting as surreptitious a glance back at Peter and Ray as I could. "How did you find the place?"

"A taxi from the train station. They did the rest," he said. "You're right. I should have called first. I'm sorry. I just ... reacted." With me having turned slightly in order to see back into the living room, Marty could now see in there as well, and it was apparent he could make out the two men in the living room behind me.

"Oh, you have company. I'm sorry. I should have been more considerate."

I shook my head. "No, no, don't be silly. Of course you're welcome here. It's just ... not the best timing, is all," I said, trying to hint by my clipped, quiet voice through clenched teeth that perhaps Marty could keep things discreet in front of the two strangers he saw behind me. The hard part, though, was going to be explaining why he was here in the first place. He and I knew precisely why he was here, but Ray and Peter didn't have a clue who this was yet.

"Come on in," I offered, stepping aside again to let Marty and his backpack into the living room. He stepped in eagerly, still smiling, although sheepishly. When I had closed the front door behind him and turned around, I saw that Peter and Ray had both stood at their spots in front of the couch and were blinking at Marty, then me, waiting for me to step up and introduce him to them. Which I did.

"Marty, these are two friends from church. This is our pastor, Ray Compton, and that's Peter Bellows at the far end of the couch. Ray, Peter, this is Marty Emerson."

One at a time, Marty extended his hand to each of the two men and shook hands with them eagerly. He was doing marvelously well for someone who was apt to ingratiate himself in a groveling fashion to just about everyone around him.

"Good to meet you," he offered to each man in turn, and each of them responded with, "Good to meet you too, Marty."

Although Ray looked perplexed about who Marty was, Peter knew. He and I had had a lot of conversations about Marty's potential conversion over the past year or so since I first started getting flyers about the class reunion. He'd seen enough pictures of Marty and had heard enough stories about the good ol' days to paint a fairly clear picture in his head about Marty and the situation between us over the years. That is, until very recently, of course.

Marty, on the other hand, knew relatively little about Peter and absolutely nothing about Ray. And he didn't know that Peter and I had been praying for him off and on for nearly a year now. Just as well. That would have raised the thorniness of the present group exponentially. And I definitely wasn't up for that. This was already a nightmare of insane proportions. In fact, if the doorbell rang one more time, this would start feeling like a bad Marx Brothers movie. One that wasn't very funny. One with all Zeppos.

Apparently just giving them Marty's name wasn't enough because Ray still looked a bit blank around the edges.

"Marty went to school with me. He's the one who was at my bedside last month after the attack."

Yes, that sounded much better than saying he was the one I'd slept with last month right before the attack. And, technically, just as true. Technically.

"Ohhh," Ray said, awareness dawning on him all at once. "So you're the one who stood guard over Emily for us." He offered his hand to Marty, and they shook hands again. "We thank you for that, Marty. We've been quite worried about her, as you can guess."

Marty nodded a lot, unsure how much Ray knew about what was going on. I could see him glancing from Ray to Peter, and back again, keeping himself from discussing The Big Topic at any depth, and I turned to see Ray doing the same thing. If I weren't so concerned about keeping my secrets, it would have been comical to watch both of these men trying to keep the same secret from each other, unaware that the other man knew a lot more than he let on. I merely shook my head and buried it in my hands, sitting in the rocking chair and trying not to look up. Peter was being strangely silent; I didn't even hear him fidgeting from his end of the couch. He was probably making some mental calculations of a nature I couldn't discern from across the room.

"Marty," I said, interrupting the disquieting stillness that had begun to settle in the room. "Have a seat in the recliner. Get comfortable."

I stood as he sat.

"Would you like some hot cocoa?" I asked hopefully, taking that first step toward the kitchen. I was beginning to think I should apply for a job at Swiss Miss. I'd look so fetching in those little braids.

"No thanks," he answered politely. "I'm fine."

I kept walking, past the three men seated in my living room, and into the kitchen, again into a haven and away from the weirdness in the next room.

I barely made it around the corner into the kitchen and out of sight of the three of them before I gasped out a sob I didn't see coming. It disturbed me enough that I closed my eyes, cupped a hand over my mouth quickly, slid down the wall next to the fridge as if on my haunches, and clutched my midsection. With the sob stifled, I opened my eyes, only to find myself staring at Marty's knees in front of me. My sob-gasp had been heard after all. Fweepit, never one to miss an opportunity to make a new lifelong friend, was already wrapping himself around Marty's legs.

Marty silently held a hand down to me, and I gratefully took it and let him help me up to standing. Without guarding myself, I looked him in the eye, lip quivering but hand still over my own mouth. He plumbed the depths of sadness on my face with those gray eyes, moist with tears and brimming with emotion, so much emotion, so much my fault.

I let my hand drop away from my mouth and threw both arms around his neck to hug him close to me, mostly in order to bury my face in his neck and sob more quietly. His arms instinctively closed around me, as he quietly breathed into my ear, "Shhhh. Hush, Em. It'll be okay ..."

Not feeling any better, I instead choked down a few more sobs, which got increasingly louder despite my best efforts to keep Ray or Peter from hearing them. Marty took to patting me on the back as he hushed me gently. I knew if I gave in now, my knees would buckle and I'd end up back on the floor if Marty couldn't hold me up, which he probably couldn't.

We stood there locked together for what seemed like ages. It was a good thing Marty wasn't waiting for me to say something because my mind was a mushy gelatinous blank. The sobs were further apart now, catching in my throat as they began to subside.

I blinked open my eyes, to see Ray and Peter blinking back at me, standing just a few feet away in the kitchen with Marty and me. In a guilty panic, I yanked myself free of Marty, who still had his back to the two other men. I pushed Marty farther away from me and stood as far back from him as seemed plausible, although this was solely a knee-jerk reaction, since Ray and Peter could have been standing in the kitchen for quite a little while for all I knew. However long they'd been there, it was at least obvious that they'd clearly seen Marty and me hugging and me crying my eyes out. What they thought of the scene was anybody's guess. But I had a feeling I was about to find out.

"Ray ... Peter," I spluttered. I held my tongue to keep from blurting out, "How long have you two been standing there?" Instead, I managed to say, "I just kinda lost it out here. Sorry."

Now all three men were standing there staring at me, none of them quite knowing what to say or do. It would be funny if they were looking to me for guidance on what came next, except that I could feel my sense of humor seeping out the bottoms of my shoes.

I wiped the last vestiges of tears from the corners of my eyes and sniffled. "Just to clear things up a little bit, Marty already knows about the *pregnancy from the attack*, just like you guys."

All three of them relaxed and let out a huge collective sigh.

"Yes," Marty acknowledged nervously. "Emily called me *days ago* to give me the news. Naturally I was as shocked as the rest of you—"

"Marty!" I interrupted hastily. "Are you sure you don't want some of that cocoa I offered you?"

Too late, though. It was out there. Peter was putting two and two together—and was getting five.

"*Days* ago?" he asked.

"Ye-ess," Marty answered hesitantly, unsure what trap he had stepped into but sure something was wrong.

"How many *days* ago?" Peter asked, clipping his words intentionally so I would notice.

Marty looked to me for help fielding this one, knowing he had stumbled into dangerous territory. Peter's addition was rapidly improving, and if I didn't hurry, soon he'd figure out about multiplying.

"Just last night, actually," I chimed in, locking eyes with Marty instead of Peter. I hoped against hope that Marty followed what I was about to say.

"I figured since Marty was there at the hospital after I was attacked, he should know about the pregnancy too. It was so nice of him to be there for me after the attack that it seemed wrong not to tell him too. So, I called him last night."

I nodded a bit exaggeratedly in Marty's direction. He looked at me blankly and, for a brief moment, I thought he hadn't followed me and was stuck back in the truth. Then I saw it dawn on him—the fact that Peter and Ray both assumed I was pregnant because of the attack. I tried not to feel guilty that I felt relieved because Marty would have no problem lying for me ... *with* me. I was going to have to skip the "And lead us not into temptation" line in the Lord's Prayer today. I was not only falling into my own temptation but I was becoming adept at dragging other people into it with me. But, I'd think about all that later. First things first. And first was extricating myself from this absurd love-triangle of men in my kitchen.

"Yeah. She called me just ... last ... night," Marty said slowly, letting each syllable ooze out of him one at a time while he looked to me for confirmation that he was heading in the right direction. I blinked a tiny nod of confirmation in his direction, hoping Ray and Peter hadn't noticed it.

"So," Marty continued, "as soon as I heard, I thought she might need some support. You know, a friendly face and stuff like that."

Ray and Peter nodded slowly, seemingly willing to go along with the story as it was currently unfolding. That was the irony of a circumstance like this: Christians often got to a point where they trusted people and believed the best in them, despite clues to the contrary.

And although many members of our congregation had problems with gossip, it was still gossip mostly in my favor. For the most part, they were willing to believe that I'd been raped. And, since I hadn't gotten to the same point of sanctification that many of my Christian friends had, I was willing to let them believe it.

I felt perspiration begin to collect in the crook of my elbows as I kept my arms crossed tightly across my chest. The back of my neck felt moist and I could feel my pulse pounding in my temples and throat. I really needed to disengage myself from this nightmare before Marty and I got in too deep to get out safely.

The more I thought about what was happening in my kitchen, and what was going to continue to happen in my life if I stayed on this path, the more sweat began to collect in my fleshly nooks and crannies. I could hear the blood whooshing in my veins, the noise of it washing in my ears along with the throbbing thumps of my heartbeat, which felt as if it had doubled its pace.

Marty was babbling on faintly in the background, presumably still filling in fake details of our phone call or the reunion or how we met or some other details no one needed to know about. Didn't matter. I couldn't hear it clearly anymore and it wasn't until I realized my field of vision was dropping that it occurred to me that my knees were buckling and I was fainting.

The room flipped upside down, went black with all-white objects in it, like a photo negative, and I never heard the thud as I hit the floor. Dramatic reactions to life had now officially become my signature.

PART THREE: CLEAR

"They whom God hath accepted in His beloved, effectually called, and sanctified by His Spirit, can neither totally, nor finally, fall away from the state of grace: but shall certainly persevere therein to the end, and be eternally saved."

— *The Westminster Confession of Faith*, 17:1

21

"Y"OU'VE GOT TO TAKE IT EASY, EM. You're under too much stress." I looked at Peter from under the warm quilt I'd pulled up to my chin. I'd been in bed for a few hours now, doing nothing but watching bad TV in the background and pondering my wildly unraveling life in the foreground.

"Peter, if I take it any easier, I'll be in an unconscious stupor." He smiled. "Again." He smiled wider.

"Glad to see the sarcasm's intact."

"Yeah, I bet."

He came to sit on the edge of the bed. I had awakened shortly after fainting—mere seconds or minutes, at most—to find that someone had already carried me to my bed. Peter was the only face looking down at me then—and now. After a while of this star-gazing, I'd asked nervously about Ray and Marty.

"Well, Ray thought maybe all of us being here at the same time was just too much for you. So we all thought it best to give you some space."

"Where's Marty?"

"He's crashing at my place for now. I gave him my keys and Ray said he'll drop him off at my apartment on his way home. Don't worry about them. The point was for you to relax and calm down."

Yeah, I was calming down, all right. Marty was bunking with Peter indefinitely and I was pregnant and fielding hardballs better than Ozzie Smith. I had every reason to calm down, didn't I?

Now, several hours later, Peter was still here with me, waiting on me hand and foot, although my hands and feet didn't need any waiting on and I really didn't need or want anything except the peace and quiet he said he wanted me to have.

"Peter, how much longer till the kids come back from Cassie's?" It was around 4:30 now and I'd taken advantage of Cassie's good graces long enough for one day.

Peter glanced at his watch. "Maybe I should call her and see if she can hold onto them a while longer."

"No," I insisted. "I want them back. It'll make me feel better. Make things feel more ... normal around here."

Peter frowned, unsure of my decision.

"Really. Call her. See when she can bring them back. I'll be all right."

"Would you like me to stay and help you out with them then?"

"No. No. We'll be fine. I think I just need to get back to normal. Or, as close to normal as I can get at this point."

I pulled myself up to sitting in the bed and let the quilt slip down to my waist. "Thanks, though, for calling her for me. That'd be great."

Peter sighed disapprovingly and walked out the bedroom door toward the stairs, casting me a backward glance that objected strenuously to my being left alone with my children. I'd done enough fainting and crying and sobbing and weeping over the past few days to make anyone with testosterone think I was a true damsel in distress. I, on the other hand, wasn't really in the market for a knight in shining armor. Not just now.

Aside from the quiet white noise of the television voices across the room, I was alone with my thoughts. I realized quite forcefully that I didn't *want* to be alone with my thoughts. I spent far too much time alone with my thoughts. I just didn't like my thoughts. I just couldn't think of anyone who would like my thoughts anymore. I just couldn't think.

22

It wasn't until Faith and Mikey were back home, curled up on my bed with me watching bad TV, that I began to feel more relaxed than I had in days. I didn't feel nauseous this evening, which was a minor miracle in itself. The earlier panic of having Ray, Peter, and Marty under the same roof simultaneously had subsided to a dull roar. I tried not to think about the baby too much. And I willed myself not to think about what kind of slumber party Marty and Peter were having over at Peter's apartment across town; that would scare the jammies off me for sure. And I was in no mood to go jammy-less tonight. I'd already done enough of that.

My bravery firmly established, I sat between Mikey and Faith and laughed with them at whatever silly show they were watching on Nickelodeon. They were glad to be home and had relaxed over the obvious cessation of hostilities in the house. It didn't matter to them what had happened here today. All they knew was that things were better. Mom was her old self again. It seemed horribly unfair that things were going to shift for them again so badly, so soon. But, for now we were at peace, and that was enough to get us through the night.

+ + + + +

THE NEXT MORNING I WOKE UP EARLY to call the office and request a personal day from work. I slipped out of bed without waking Faith and Mikey—who had stayed there with me because I hadn't the heart to move them after they fell asleep so soundly and easily—and tiptoed downstairs to make my phone call.

While in the kitchen, I grabbed the dangling address book next to the phone and quickly found Marty's cell phone number. The ink probably wasn't dry yet on the number, which I got from Marty while I was in the hospital last month. As I dialed his area code, I remembered that Marty was in Peter's apartment. Even if Marty was awake this early, I couldn't guarantee that he'd be able to take the call privately, or that Peter wouldn't hear the ring and ask about it afterwards. It just didn't look good for me to call Marty first thing in the morning. I desperately needed to talk to him—alone—but this wasn't the way to do it. Until I was sure Peter had gone to work and Marty was alone, I had to restrain myself and not call Peter or Marty.

This feeling that things just *happened* to me—things beyond my control yet incredibly pivotal—deepened. I opened the fridge and took out the metal canister of coffee. A little caffeine would do wonders for my disposition. Just a little, though, with the pregnancy, so I opened the fridge again and took out the canister of decaf as well. Might as well be a good girl in at least one area of my life.

The smell of the brewing coffee was delightful and I stood in the kitchen breathing it in for a moment longer. The clock above the sink clicked over to 8:00, and still the kids were zonked. Nick at Nite was a lifesaver for keeping the kids and me up late last night.

I poured myself a mug of the swiss chocolate java I'd just brewed and stood looking out the side window near the stove. What time would Peter be leaving for work—for sure? No way of knowing, really. I didn't know much about his daily routine in the morning and hadn't a clue when he was expected at work or when he left to get there. I'd have to wait for Marty to call here or risk calling Peter's home number and talking to him first if he was still home. No way of knowing what to do, and no way of truly feeling at ease about it all until I talked to Marty. That might not be for hours.

Closing my eyes and sipping the steaming coffee, I vowed not to let this unsettle me. This was just a minor setback. The worst of it was over.

As I swallowed another sweet mouthful of coffee, I heard a faint rapping noise. At first I thought it was just some sort of animal or bird outside the house, scratching on something. But it came again: tap, tap, tap. Too deliberate and rhythmic to be a squirrel. There was someone quietly knocking on the front door, only wanting to be heard if someone was relatively near the door. Which I was. I stepped silently toward the door, coffee cup still in hand, thinking that maybe I'd look into putting in a revolving door to accommodate the ridiculous amount of foot traffic lately. For all I knew, this person was knocking because the doorbell had finally worn out. I went to the window to the right of the front door and pushed aside the slats of the mini-blinds enough to peek out.

There stood Marty, fidgeting on my front porch, randomly tapping on his cell phone with one hand and running the other hand through his thin hair nervously. I let the slats fall back together, unlatched the door, and opened it. He abruptly stopped his fiddling and looked up at me and grinned.

"Emily, hi!"

"Marty, come in," I offered and stood back from the door to allow him to get past me. He put his phone in his coat pocket and came into the house. I closed the door quietly and followed him into the living room. Although he'd been in this room just the day before, he stood there looking out of place and unsure what to do next.

"Please, sit down," I said, gesturing to the couch and heading for the rocking chair myself.

"Are you okay? How are you feeling?" he asked as he sat. "I wanted to call from Peter's house but didn't think that was such a good idea, given the situation."

"I was thinking the same thing, which is why I didn't call you either. I'm fine. I just needed some good, old-fashioned rest and some quality time with the kids. I'm feeling much better."

Marty's eyes darted around the room nervously. "Speaking of your kids, where are they? Are they here?" He didn't look particularly eager to meet them.

"They're asleep. We were up late last night watching TV together, just kind of cuddling up and hanging loose."

"Oh, okay. Good." I tried not to take umbrage at that, and I must have looked particularly offended because he stood and smiled warmly.

"No, I didn't mean it that way," he said, coming over to me in the rocking chair and getting down on his knees on the wooden floor to be eye to eye with me. "I just wanted to hug you without a bunch of little eyes watching me."

And he did just that. Hugged me. Awkwardly, to be honest, because the rocking chair came forward when he wrapped his arms around me and I nearly tumbled into his arms. We both laughed noiselessly as he stayed crouched before me, rubbing my back lightly, comfortingly. I sighed openly.

"Everything's going to be okay, Em. Honest."

I laughed again. "I don't know how you can know that. You have no idea what all this involves. What it means in my life."

He pulled back from the embrace to look at me. "True, but you're not alone in this. I want to help you out."

I wasn't sure if he was being chivalrous—which was the most natural explanation, given Marty's proclivities regarding women—or offensively naive. Opting for the first interpretation, I patted him under the chin maternally.

"I'm going to need the help, that's for sure."

"I mean it. Money. Time. I was even thinking maybe I could move and find a job here to be closer to you and the baby."

I blinked but said nothing. Marty seemed to pick up on my balking.

"If that's okay with you, of course." He looked confused by my lack of reaction to his offer to move closer.

"Oh, it's not that, Marty. Of course I'd rather have you here than far away. I meant other kinds of help too. Help with trying to explain to everyone what happened ... and what didn't happen. They all think this is because of the mugging."

"So they don't know about us at all yet?" Thankfully, he didn't sound upset that I hadn't told the whole world about him when I got back into town after being released from the hospital.

"No. I was trying to forget it ever happened, and just about when I started to think it was going to go away, I found out I was pregnant. And before I got used to the idea myself, everyone else accidentally found out I was pregnant, too. That was just the other day. I haven't had time to sit back and deal with all of this myself, and now I have to deal with everyone else too."

He got up off his knees and went back to the couch, probably because it couldn't have been at all comfortable kneeling on my hardwood floor for that long.

"I guess I just don't understand what the big deal is. You just tell everyone you're having a baby, and they learn to deal with it. If they can't, that's their problem, not yours. Right?"

"You don't understand how this works. It's not as easy as that. There are ... rules," I said, for lack of a better word.

"But those are their rules, not yours. Just ignore them."

"No, you still don't understand. They're my rules too. That's how it works when you become a member of a church. You take vows."

"Vows? Like being married? You can't be serious. I mean, membership rules are one thing, but this sounds downright ... oppressive. They shouldn't be able to suffocate you like that, and make you worry about something that you can't change."

"I can't change things now, but I could have changed things before it got this complicated, and wrong. That's the point, Marty, and I agree with them on that point. This was a mistake, a *sin*."

He began vigorously shaking his head.

"I know you don't like that word, but it's true. At least in my world it is. It's something I'm going to have to confront and own up to. And I'm mostly fine with that, but right now I'm feeling a little overwhelmed with the morning sickness and everyone finding out all at once. It's too soon after the attack. The bruises just went away about a week go."

He winced. I leaned back in the rocking chair and began rocking rapidly. A wash of emotion made my heart flutter unexpectedly, and I felt my bottom lip quivering. I was going to lose it.

"That's what I mean," Marty continued. "You have so much on your plate already. Can't these people cut you a little slack?" He was beginning to sound perturbed.

"They're not *doing* anything to me, Marty. No one has said anything directly to me yet. I'm just running worst-case scenarios in my head. And I keep telling myself that they just live slightly more sheltered lives than maybe you and your friends are used to. But that's not a bad thing."

Perhaps I was going a little far defending them, but Marty truly was misreading their motives in this.

"Emily, they're being kind to you now because they all think you were raped. How are they going to react once they find out you weren't?"

I kept rocking, trying to work off the adrenaline I felt building up the more we talked.

"They'll be rightly shocked. They'll probably think Peter is the father."

That halted the conversation dead in its tracks. Mention of Peter in a context that reminded Marty that Peter was officially my significant other disturbed him. Seems Marty had momentarily forgotten that he didn't have me all to himself.

"Peter? That guy wouldn't sin if his life depended on it," he said sarcastically.

I thought about that for a moment, and said wistfully, "You're probably right."

"So, once these people find out you're a sinner, what do you think they'll do to you?"

"They won't do anything to me. And, they already know I'm a sinner. We all are. So are you. So is Peter. No news there. Listen, Marty, it's a lot more complicated than I can explain in a few minutes. Nobody's out to get me"—I thought briefly about Everett Newman as soon as I said that—"but I will have to be accountable for what happened."

He was frowning deeply. "It's just not right."

"Just because we draw our lines in different places doesn't mean we're acting any different than the rest of society. If your definition of sin runs a little more into the category of truly evil, then you'd probably want the same sorts of consequences and accountability at *that* level instead of this one. It's really not any different in theory."

I heard myself saying things I didn't even realize I believed enough to defend. Hearing sound doctrine come out of my mouth, especially at a time like this, while Marty was soaking it in, astonished me. I was never very good at proselytizing anyone, let alone someone who meant as much to me as Marty. Often I didn't want to risk the disapproval and ostracism of someone I'd come to depend on. And I'd seen it happen to nicer people than I.

But this time Marty was attacking my chosen way of life. I wasn't witnessing to him so much as I was defending myself. The line between the two had become a little blurry for me. I was taking what Marty was saying a little too personally.

I self-consciously rubbed my lower tummy and let myself think about the baby. I didn't feel scared. I didn't feel overwhelmed or sad. I just felt quietly resigned and maybe a little excited. I so loved being pregnant, and I particularly adored newborn babies. They were warm, cuddly, smelled wonderful, and made the best little grunting noises while they were trying merely to adjust to existence in the real world.

A baby. A new baby. When I stopped to think about it—I mean, really stopped, really slowed down and stopped—I knew this could be an amazing opportunity and was already a blessing in disguise. Life, after so much death.

I smiled while I continued to rub my tummy, rocking lightly now, peacefully. Before I realized what I was doing, I started humming a little too.

"Emily? You okay?"

My trance broken, I stopped my methodical rubbing, looked up from my tummy and at Marty. The poor guy was more confused than when he first showed up. I must have seemed like a basket case with my emotional waffling. I flashed him a smile. He deserved one for putting up with me.

"Yeah, I'm fine. I was just allowing myself a few minutes to think about the baby."

He was smiling back at me. "Well, good. I'm glad thinking about the baby makes you smile. Now, what next?"

Like all men—even emotional men like Marty—his pragmatic side had kicked in. It was time to diagnose the problem and fix it, to roll up our sleeves and get to work somehow.

"I have to call my OB/GYN and make an appointment. And I have to make an appointment with ... Ray." I said the name slowly and quietly, not wanting to admit in front of Marty that my pastor was on the short list of baby-related appointments along with my obstetrician. He wouldn't understand.

"Ray? The pastor?"

"I have to tell him the truth. He has to know. If I start with him, maybe he'll be able to help me figure out a way to tell Peter and everybody else. You just moving here and showing up at my house all the time isn't the way to go about doing this."

"Why not?"

"I have to dot my *i*'s and cross my *t*'s. Don't worry about it. It's just something I know I have to do. So I'll be able to sleep at night ... eventually."

He was shaking his head again. Standing again, he paced around to the front of the coffee table and stopped in front of the mantelpiece. On it I kept framed photos of Faith and Mikey, and even one of Fweepit: Faith in a little tutu, Mikey with Faith in their jammies around the tree last Christmas, Faith and Mikey holding Fweepit on their laps in the rocking chair, barely enough room for the three of them. Marty's eyes moved from one photo to the next, taking in what he could understand of my life—so different from his own, I knew. The contrast was starker with him standing in my house, in my living room, in front of pictures of my children.

Suddenly, as if his watching Faith and Mikey in framed three-by-fives made them come to life, we heard their scurrying footfalls on the carpeted stairs. To me it was a comforting, familiar sound, but to Marty I could see it set him on edge. He stood up straight, cleared his throat loudly, and turned away from the photos and toward the stair-way behind the couch, awaiting their appearance at the bottom with a kind of trepidation I didn't recognize.

"Mom! Are you down here?" came the voice of Faith from the stairway. Then, as soon as she'd said that, she appeared around the corner and kept running, spotting me in my familiar place in the rocking chair. Marty followed her path all the way across the room in a shocked sort of daze, but Faith never noticed him, instead making her beeline for me without taking her eyes off me.

"Hi, sweets!" I said, arms outstretched to swoop her in. She hugged me fiercely as I watched Mikey coming up behind her, look-ing askance at Marty as he toddled over. He stopped about ten feet from us, turning to face Marty from the other side of the couch.

"Mommy, who this?" He pointed bluntly at Marty, no social grac-es whatsoever about the rudeness of pointing.

Faith broke free from hugging me and turned first toward Mikey, and then toward where he was pointing. Her eyes widened as she saw a stranger standing by the mantelpiece. She immediately turned to me for an explanation, which I fully intended to fudge on giving her. Well, which I intended to truncate, anyway.

"This is a friend of mine, Marty Emerson. I went to school with him when I was growing up."

Marty grinned sheepishly from his place beside the mantel, then waved like a cartoon character atop a parade float.

"Hi, kids!"

Faith and Mikey looked at each other, then looked at Marty, then turned to me, eyes pleading.

"Say hello, guys!" I said cheerily, hoping they would be typical kids and grunt out a hello and then leave Marty alone out of boredom. Meanwhile, Marty continued his exaggerated wave from across the room.

"Hi," they both said, emotionless and suddenly uninterested. This was just some old guy their mother knew. He hadn't even brought them presents. Nothing worth sticking around for.

"C'mon, Mikey," Faith announced, holding her hand out for her brother. "Let's go get some Cheerios." He dutifully took her hand and allowed himself to be led toward the kitchen. Faith gave me a backward glance, and I nodded at her Cheerios suggestion. Neat, clean, and easy to reach since I started putting the box in a lower cabinet instead of one above the counter.

When they were out of the living room, I looked back around, only to see Marty sitting on the floor in front of the mantel, his head in his hands. His hands were visibly shaking, and he seemed close to hyperventilating. Apparently it had all become just a tad too real for him.

"Marty! Are you all right?" I asked as I rose out of the rocking chair and went to him.

"No," he admitted. "Dear God, no."

23

LTHOUGH I FEARED THE WORST WITH MARTY, he managed to avoid fainting dead away in my living room. Apparently we couldn't *both* be melodramatic. I helped him get up and back onto the couch, where he continued to hang his head low in an effort to keep his blood flowing and his consciousness from ebbing. He looked terribly pale, and I offered him the possibility of some Cheerios in hopes of helping him gain his equilibrium. He wasn't interested. Probably too big a reminder of the wee ones sitting a few feet away in the kitchen.

We both knew that Faith and Mikey being awake and alert meant the serious parts of our conversation had to be curtailed. He began eyeing the door and the clock not long after sinking down onto the couch. He reached into his pocket and pulled out his cell phone, fiddling with it uneasily.

"Marty, maybe we'll have to continue this sometime later, when the kids aren't around listening."

He nodded. A lot. And he began to tap the phone screen, then held it up to his ear.

"Peter? This is Marty. Can you come pick me up at Emily's? I'm not feeling all that great." Peter said something and Marty chuckled anxiously. "Heh heh. Contagious. Yeah, maybe. She looks better, and I feel worse. Could be." Peter said something else. "Okay, I'll be ready. Thanks."

Marty ended the call and put the phone back into his pocket before looking my way.

"*Peter* brought you here?" I asked, dumbfounded.

"Yes, of course. How did you think I got here?"

"I hadn't really thought about it. You just kinda showed up. I hadn't been awake all that long. It's ... early."

+ + + + +

WITHIN TWENTY MINUTES THE DOORBELL RANG AGAIN, and I knew that it was Peter. The kids were upstairs watching bad TV in my bed, without me this time, and Marty and I had kept a vigil for Peter downstairs in the living room, speaking in hushed tones. When the doorbell rang, Marty stood and headed unceremoniously for the door. I followed him and held the door open as he moved toward the porch. He turned in the doorway and faced me, standing close. I looked past him, to Peter's car in the driveway. Peter didn't get out of his car, merely let the car idle while waiting for Marty to come out, and I instinctively pulled back from the doorway enough to keep from being seen.

Marty sighed and reached out to touch my arm. I flinched imperceptibly.

"Emily, I'll call you when I can get alone somewhere."

He still looked pale. Babies grew up into little kids—like the ones he'd met in my house. In fact, in this case, a *lot* like the ones in my house. If I was having trouble with the concept, how much more jolting was it for Marty?

I got up the nerve to pat him on the forearm. "Just don't throw up in Peter's car. He wouldn't like that."

Marty chortled in spite of himself. "Okay, I won't."

I retreated into the house and watched from the side window as Marty walked around to the passenger side of Peter's car and got in. Peter threw his arm over the passenger seat and backed his car out of the driveway as I watched, hidden safely in the shadows by the window. It was the height of freaky to watch Peter drive Marty away from my house after a semi-clandestine meeting to discuss our baby. Suddenly I felt the way Marty looked.

"Mom! Mikey's crying about the TV again! He won't let me watch *SpongeBob!*"

My shoulders sagged and some confused weariness seeped into my pores.

"Okay, hon. I'm on my way up!" I assured her, turning away from the window and slogging toward the stairs. The fun just never ended at the Saunders house.

+ + + + +

I CLIMBED BACK INTO BED, both Mikey and Faith giggling with glee at Mom joining them back in bed—after breakfast.

They curled up on either side of me, settling in quietly and quickly, which told me they still hadn't had enough sleep from last night. I grabbed the remote off the headboard and turned the sound down a little on the TV, hoping they'd drift back to sleep and let me think some things through in peace.

I soon heard regular breathing on both my left and my right, and I ignored the TV in favor of daydreaming about babies. Without realizing it, I started by daydreaming about my very first baby, who was now sleeping peacefully at my side. My own breathing became hauntingly regular.

+ + + + +

"EMILY, DON'T PUSH!" MY MIDWIFE HAD URGED. "Gennntle—nice and gentle—blow through this."

She was right. It burned.

I thought, *This burns like hell*, and then my mind added, *literally. This must be what hell feels like, only all over.*

Surprisingly, the pain itself didn't really bother me; it was the thought of what might happen to me if I gave in to the unbearable urge to push. The very idea of torn flesh—*my* flesh, in perhaps the single most vulnerable place on my body—terrified me. It had been my one recurring fear throughout my entire pregnancy.

A familiar voice faintly reached my ears from miles away, far off in the distance.

"Emmy, look!" It was Jonathan.

I opened my eyes, which I didn't remember closing, and instantly traveled the miles back to the bedroom. Both Jon and Liz, the midwife, were perspiring heavily; I initially thought they were crying, but then focused in on the beads of moisture on both their foreheads. I didn't dare to think what I must have looked like after, what? Was it a full twenty-four hours of labor now? I couldn't remember what it felt like *not* to be in labor.

"Emily, look," Liz said. She was smiling at me and holding up a mirror for me to view the goings-on. I looked into it before I realized exactly what I'd see. Instinctively I turned away from the sight of a huge head bulging, *bulging*, trying desperately to push my body to the limit. It looked worse than it felt.

"No," I groaned softly. "Take it away. ... It's too much."

Liz dropped the mirror onto the edge of the bed and took over from Jon the job of applying counter-pressure on my stretching perineal tissue.

"Okay, Emily, just blow through this next contraction, and I think we'll have the head."

It seemed impossible. Everything began rushing in on me. The contraction appeared out of nowhere and peaked early. I had no time to get on top of it.

"What should I do? What should I do? Tell me!" I begged. If she had told me to whistle "Dixie," I would have asked her what key she wanted.

"Blow! Blow! Don't push!"

Jonathan scrambled onto the bed and planted himself right in my face. He began modeling his breathing for me, blowing little puffs of air rapidly in my face. *Onions, onions.* The hoagie from last night. *Onions.* I tried to blow back at him. Out of the corner of my eye, my heightened senses noticed that Liz, hands still firmly molding my tissues around a head the size of a basketball, grimaced ever so slightly. "Above all," she added quickly, "don't tighten up. Relax!"

Sure. Absolutely had to be the stupidest thing I had ever heard. Whistling "Dixie" would have made more sense.

Jonathan blew harder and faster in my face and I blinked several times.

"Sorry, hon," he offered, and I looked squarely at him. I had never, until that moment, seen real fear in Jon's eyes. But, there it was—fear—and it had taken over his entire face. Every muscle, every drop of sweat, every pore had fear carved in it.

"I'm sorry," he repeated, sounding embarrassed and guilt-ridden. I could easily see every thought in his head then, and it made me weak to see it all. Jonathan wasn't afraid of being a father, or of feeding and clothing a new family member, or even of losing what little privacy we had enjoyed up until that point. He was scared senseless for the baby, and, more immediately, for me. He had absolutely no idea what was really happening to me, and it was destroying him to see me from across so great a chasm. He had no advice to give, no Scripture to quote, no platitude big enough to cover this.

He was confronting a form of death for the first time, up close and personal, and he had nothing to say, nothing to offer. In our fear we both saw death then—just inches and moments before we saw life—and it was a hungry, gnawing monster as big as the universe and as wide as time. It was nibbling at our toes, and we stared into each other's souls for an instant. It was the most horrible and intimate moment I had ever shared with anyone.

"Blow! Blow!" Liz's voice sliced through it all, and the death monster popped out of sight, like a disappearing blip on a radar screen. I had stopped blowing and was holding my breath and unknowingly tightening every muscle in my body.

"Relax, dammit!" Liz yelled.

Jonathan began blowing frantically in my face again, and perched himself next to me so he could stroke my arms lightly to get me to relax. It worked where words would have failed miserably. I blew out the tension and tightening in tiny spurts, and I conquered the urge to grab the sheets and bear down again, just one last time.

"Jon ..." I gasped between blows of air, "my hands feel all tingly."

Liz didn't look up from her artful perineal massage. "Jonathan, get her to slow down—now!"

Jonathan halved his blows immediately, and soon I had picked up his new pattern. The tingling subsided. But, the burning returned. *Fire, fire.* Tight little rims of fire, so precise, so well-defined, so intense ... a branding iron, a circle of scorching coals searing out from my body ... stretch, stretch ... *God, don't let my bottom split open, no, no, no ...*

"Don't fight it, Emily. Let it happen! Let this baby out. It's all right. You're fine. He'll fit."

I grasped this truth, and clung to it, letting go of everything else. I felt my body erupt. Suddenly, all the burning smoldered away in one unexpected and welcome blip. I was too frightened to look at myself, but I heard a shrill squeak from Jonathan and then the gurgly noises of the bulb syringe Liz had just grabbed off the end table with one hand.

"Emmy, you should see all the hair!" In the midst of my sensory confusion, I assumed he meant my pubic hair.

"What?"

"The baby! A full head of hair!"

The baby! I tried to right myself a bit from my semi-sitting position to get a glimpse of the head, but to no avail.

Liz issued more instructions. "Emily, you'll feel the baby turning 90 degrees so the rest of the body can slip out. This next contraction is just as important as the last couple. Jonathan, keep her blowing through these, so the bottom shoulder doesn't drag."

Jonathan reluctantly tore his gaze away from the baby's head and clambered back up to my side. The contraction didn't wait for him, and I was too impatient to pay attention to his annoying and persistent panting in my face. Thoughts of the baby—*the baby!*—pushed and shoved their way past my preoccupation with my abused flesh and planted themselves firmly in the front of my consciousness.

There was no pressure now, just the acute sensation of a large, oddly shaped body still inside my own. It turned, with God's help not mine, and, with Liz's hands still managing my perineum, the rest of the baby slipped wet out of my body. I felt it slide noiselessly onto the bed.

"A girl," Jonathan sighed. His voice was quivering and he was about to fall apart.

She lay face up, all four limbs flailing in a quiet panic, her large hazy eyes blinking repeatedly. *There is a God, there is a God ...*

In a rush of insight so tangible I swear it pulsed in my veins, I knew God to be wholly sovereign, in a way only a laboring woman can fathom. I felt simultaneously all-important and embarrassingly insignificant. Even after hours of sensory overload and the grueling strain of childbirth, I realized that this had everything and nothing to do with me. God's eternal and unsearchable purpose was woven into this event, as it was in all such moments.

Perhaps thirty seconds had passed since the birth, no more. I watched as Liz pulled out the receiving blanket she had been storing under her own shirt for warmth and covered the baby. Then, with the infinite gentleness of someone who respected this juncture with every ounce of her being, Liz lay the helpless new being on my sweaty, trembling abdomen.

"Put your hand under the blanket and massage her back," Liz whispered.

I did as I was told, still not quite aware of the reality of our bedroom, nor the big wide world outside it.

"Yeah, that's right. Get that circulation going good."

Jonathan rubbed my hand from outside the blanket in a feeble effort to be as much a part of this as he possibly could. I barely felt a part of it all myself. It was too colossal an experience to have been mine.

Liz's eyes barely left my bottom, still trickling blood, as she began to collect the disposable underpads spread out on the bed around my legs and feet.

"Lift your butt, gal," she said, and I dutifully complied, feeling my leg muscles shake violently as I hoisted myself a gargantuan inch or two off the bed. Liz deftly gathered up the two underpads that were there, exposing two dry, fresh ones underneath.

"Is this shaking normal?" I asked, a little worried at my inability to curb it.

"Yep. Release of hormones at the moment of birth. Perfectly normal. How ya feeling otherwise?" she asked softly.

I smiled. No, I grinned, a stupid, uncontrollable grin. "I'm super. She's great. You're great."

I turned my face up to Jon's and we kissed. "And you, well, you're not so bad either."

"Shucks, ma'am," he gushed, blinking.

Liz began prodding and poking around my traumatized perineum, a definite interruption of the moment. I winced. "Looks like no stitches for you, kiddo. You did it."

"Really?" I asked, not daring to believe it.

"You sound surprised. I told you it was possible."

"Yeah, but—"

"Yeah, but you didn't believe me, did you?" she asked.

"I won't have to see the inside of a hospital after all." She smiled, and turned her attention back to the birth canal. She reached up to my abdomen, slid her hand gently under the baby, and firmly massaged my belly. I felt it tighten.

"Sorry if this smarts a little. Just trying to get this uterus to clamp down and get this placenta out."

"It's fine," I assured her. I continued to count the baby's fingers and toes, to feel the pasty white vernix covering her warm back, to stare with awe at her fascinating, delicate features. There was enough to do here to keep me busy for days, weeks.

Liz glanced up fleetingly at the baby, who sneezed a funny little sneeze and let out an unconvincing cry. "Good. Clear out those lungs, little girl." Liz looked up to me. "Who is this little princess, by the way?" she asked.

I looked at Jonathan, who simply nodded.

"Faith," I said.

"That's pretty. So nice and old fashioned."

It was pretty. We had picked it out months ago, but hadn't known till that day just how poignant a testimony it was. She was certainly nothing if not a result of God's faithfulness to us personified.

+ + + + +

WITH THESE REASSURING MEMORIES FLOATING AROUND in the front of my psyche anew, I fell asleep next to Faith and Mikey. I remembered thinking what a great feeling it was to be curled up with them here, safe and away from the world's troubles, as I drifted into a sound sleep.

I was startled awake by Mikey crying loudly on one side of me and Faith screaming on the other side.

"Mom! *Mom!* We're dying! We're all dying!"

24

I SAT STRAIGHT UP IN THE BED, looking first at Faith and then
Mikey, disoriented and unsure how we were all dying when everything felt fine. In a split second I ascertained that the TV was
still on, the house wasn't on fire, and we weren't in the middle of a
terrorist attack in the backyard. With all that affirmed, I saw with
horror that Faith's pajamas had splotches of blood on them. Fresh
blood. I grabbed her pajama top where the blood was and felt it was
wet. Panicked, I turned to the wailing Mikey, whose pajama top was
also bloody and damp. Other than the yelling, though, they seemed
uninjured.

It wasn't until I saw Faith pointing at my lap that I looked down at
myself and saw the source of the blood. I was hemorrhaging.

"We're dying, Mom! What's happening to us?" Faith was genuinely scared, and I clutched her shoulder in a pathetic effort to comfort
her. I think I scared her instead because she shrank from my grabbing.

"Faith, it's not you. You and Mikey are fine. Honest. *I'm* bleeding,
not you."

She caught herself in mid-scream and looked at me. This option
hadn't occurred to her.

"You were just in the same bed with me when I started bleeding."
She pointed at my lap again.

"Mom! Why are you bleeding? You're dying!"

Mikey's sobbing continued. He was inconsolable, too young to to be talked out of his panic. He didn't know what dying was, but he was obviously sure it couldn't be good.

"Faith! You and Mikey are fine! I'll be fine too. Go get me the cordless phone from the dresser!"

Amid my anxiety I somehow issued proper instructions, and amid her own anxiety, Faith somehow obeyed. She slid off the bed, holding her wet pajama top out from her body to keep it from touching her skin, and ran in a tiptoe over to the dresser. She swiped the phone off the top with her other hand and ran back to me, holding the phone out in front of her.

I flicked it on and hit 9-1-1 as quickly as I could, my pulse pounding in my ears and Mikey's yowling throbbing in my heart.

+ + + + +

HOSPITALS HAD NEVER BEEN MY FAVORITE PLACES on the planet, and West Side General in particular was my least favorite. Hospitals meant death, mutilation, and disease. And, the two experiences I'd had with hospitals lately hadn't done anything to dispel that impression. In fact, they only served to solidify in my mind what I'd always known: People who go into hospitals come out changed. And not necessarily for the better.

I went into that hospital knowing what was happening to me. After calling 9-1-1, I dialed up Liz, my midwife, although she didn't even know yet that I was pregnant again. She told me over the phone what I already suspected: that I was probably having a miscarriage. While on the phone with her I felt sharp pains in my abdomen, enough to double me over completely on the bed. Faith and Mikey were beside themselves with anxiety, and there was little I could do to quell their rising panic.

My third phone call was to Meg, for her to come get the kids. She arrived while the emergency workers were making sure I was stable and cleaning me up. After my phone calls, I'd calmly instructed Faith to get clean clothing for herself and Mikey, and she'd gotten herself dressed in short order, then helped Mikey pull the pajama top off over his head. She handed him a clean T-shirt and told him in her best little-mommy voice to put it on. He was too stunned and confused to be contrary.

The next thing I knew they were off with Meg, covered in my kisses and reassurances that I would be fine as soon as the doctors got to take a look at me and give me some medicine. And I was heading for another hospital.

25

I HAD THE OVERWHELMING FEELING I'D CRIED ENOUGH for one lifetime. Liz, my midwife, was sitting in a chair next to the hospital
bed, trying her best to console me, but there were too many things
to cry about for her to make a dent in it all. Despite her enormous
stores of empathy—which were mostly responsible for her continued
success as a midwife—I became decidedly more distraught. I'd been
given the green light to pack up my things and recuperate at home,
and I desperately wanted to leave the hospital as soon as possible and
go home. But instead, I sat in the hospital bed sobbing, Liz trying to
coax me to get dressed, with no success.

After an hour of her gentle cajoling, I knew it was time to make
myself get moving and get out of there. When she asked me again
whether I wanted to go home, this time I nodded and she sprung into
action. She retrieved my clothes out of the hanging closet next to the
bathroom and brought them to me. Meg had managed to throw a
complete set of clean, fresh clothes into a plastic shopping bag for me
before she took the kids with her, and I was now grateful for her fore-
sight. Liz helped me as needed, and I slowly swung my feet over the
side of the bed and slipped to the floor onto wobbly legs. She grabbed

me and steadied me as I found my sea legs and motioned that I'd like
to visit the bathroom before going home.

"Wait," Liz said, and I turned to see her rifling through things in
the end table. She turned back to me and handed me an individually
wrapped maxi-pad, which I took gratefully before shuffling in mea-
sured steps to the bathroom.

"Shall I help you?" she called after me.

"No," I said, waving my hand back at her dismissively. "I need to
make sure I can handle things on my own if I'm going home."

"Fair enough," she agreed, packing up the few other things I had
with me while I took care of myself in the bathroom.

+ + + + +

LIZ WAS DISCREET AND TACTFUL ENOUGH to wait till we were in my
house before she brought up the indelicate subject looming over us.
I was safely planted in my trusty rocking chair, with an afghan my
grandmother had crocheted laid gently across my lap, remote control
in my hand. I was ready to engulf my brain in electronic mush, but
Liz had other ideas. She sat on the couch and inched forward to the
edge.

"Emily, I can fill in the blanks here. You don't need to say anything. I just want to know if you're going to be all right. Is there someone to take care of you?"

I looked up at her and steeled myself to answer without crying.

"Sometimes I think there are too many people ready to take care
of me. Other times I feel all alone. Depends on how I feel on any
given morning when I wake up." I bit my lip.

"The father. What about him? Will he be around to help you?"

"Help me with what?" I asked sharply. "There isn't any baby to
worry about anymore." I choked back a sob but wasn't entirely suc-
cessful.

"Still, you'll need some moral support for a while. This isn't going
to be an easy thing to recover from. Not on top of everything else."

I sighed. "I know. I'm just not ready to think about all that yet. I have too many other things to think about first. My kids are probably going bonkers over at Meg's house."

Liz smiled. "Kids bounce back pretty easily. As soon as they see you're going to be all right, they'll relax and get back into the swing of things. You have enough to worry about. I'm sure Faith and Michael will be all right."

A few minutes of silence ensued, and I rocked slowly in the chair waiting for Liz to speak.

"Aren't you going to ask me how I got into this mess?" I finally asked, unwilling to wait out the awkward lull any longer.

"No, I didn't really think it was my place to push the issue right now. I figured you'd tell me when you wanted me to know, and that that might not be today."

"Well, good. Except that I think I need someone outside of the situation to talk to about all this. Everyone else is either directly involved or is around me so much that I'm too embarrassed to be in the same room with them now."

Liz must have noticed the tears forming in my eyes and spilling onto my cheeks because she silently handed me the box of tissues from the coffee table. I set it in my lap gratefully, and took one tissue out to dab my eyes and face dry.

"You know I'm a good listener."

"I know. It's kinda what you do best."

She inched a little farther forward on the couch and clasped her hands together, laying them on her knees.

"I'm listening. Say what you need to say."

With Liz's imprimatur, I poured the whole convoluted story out for her to hear, and in the process went through most of the box of tissues. Liz, my midwife, my friend, my confessor. My first real confessor. And long overdue at that.

26

THE HOUSE WAS QUIET AGAIN. Everett Newman had left for work minutes earlier, as he usually did. Janie had seen him off with a hearty breakfast, a small show of faith in him despite what she'd learned about his past. She was incredibly tired from too little sleep lately but knew she wouldn't be able to nap with all that was on her mind right now. She needed Everett to leave for work as usual so that she could do what needed to be done.

And now she was alone in the house, alone with her thoughts and reactions. For the first time in thirty-two years, she was afraid of her husband. The man she thought of as a gruff teddy bear had perhaps just been in a long hibernation. She left the dishes in the sink and walked into the dining room, collapsing into one of the oak chairs around the pedestal table. Her hands shook uncontrollably and her heart pounded in her chest. Surely she was still asleep, still working through a nightmare. Surely this wasn't really happening.

Looking around the dining room and out the window to the street outside, though, Janie realized that it all really had happened. And she was the only one prepared to do anything about it. Her resolve finally solidified, she stood and went back into the kitchen, lifting the wall phone's receiver with shaky hands. With a deep breath to calm her nerves, she dialed the police number posted on the little whiteboard next to the phone.

+ + + + +

IT WAS ANOTHER PAPERWORK DAY FOR EVERETT, which meant he was chained to his desk fielding phone calls and catching up on project forms and calculations. He preferred days out on site, but he had seen fewer of those as he got older. Today he had little to distract him from replaying his recent confession to Janie over and over. He couldn't tell from her reaction these past few weeks—or lack of it—whether or not she believed his absurd story, whether or not she would call a psychiatrist and have him committed pronto. It was a good sign that she had gotten up with him the next morning after a fitful night's sleep and made him a hot breakfast, even kissing his cheek before he left the house. She'd gotten up and made him a cooked breakfast every morning since, and hadn't missed an opportunity to plant a buss on his cheek each day. He was wrong to worry about having told her everything. He was wrong not to have told her sooner.

Amid his musing, there was a huge commotion stirring around the elevator across the large open room. Three uniformed police officers stepped off the elevator, talked to the first person they saw, and then collectively looked in Everett's direction. No, this definitely didn't bode well, though Everett wasn't sure what he should do. There wasn't anywhere to go; his desk sat on the far side of the room, one whole corner away from the stairwell. Besides, what if he was just feeling paranoid? They could be here to collect a company donation for the policemen's ball. It did no good to panic unnecessarily.

As he talked himself into staying calm, the three men in uniform strode closer, hands covering the weapons at their sides. Before Everett had long enough to calculate a response to what he now knew was inevitable, the men were surrounding his desk in a highly intimidating fashion.

"Mr. Everett Newman?" one of the officers asked.

Everett noticed their stance and answered abjectly, "Yes. That's me." It was clear Janie had panicked and called the authorities.

The first officer spoke firmly. "You're under arrest for the assault and attempted murder of Emily Saunders."

The second officer took a pair of handcuffs off his belt and held them aloft for Everett to see, and Everett obediently held his hands out for the man to cuff him.

The third officer began a chant he'd probably said a thousand times: "You have the right to remain silent ..."

Everett Newman had no intention of remaining silent. It was time for this to be over. Maybe they had medications for whatever was wrong with him. Maybe he would be allowed to take them. He felt the handcuffs snap closed on his wrists, a little more tightly than he would have liked, and let himself be led back to the elevator, his co-workers gawking at him as if he were a circus freak.

In some ways, he thought, perhaps that was just what he had become. He'd let his anger issues—part head injury, part heart injury—simmer for far too long. He thought of Janie reading about this in the newspaper, of Janie making him breakfast earlier that morning, kissing him before he left for work, and he broke down and cried all the way across the room and into the elevator.

It is finished, he thought to himself amid his tears.

27

Q. 14. *What is sin?*

A. Sin is any want of conformity unto, or transgression of, the law of God.

— *The Westminster Shorter Catechism,* Question 14

THE NEXT MONTH PASSED QUICKLY FOR ME in some respects. I took some time off work to recuperate, catch my breath, and work out a few things. The first few days home from the hospital were chaotic—physically and emotionally. Liz was right about the kids: Faith and Mikey ran from Meg's car into the house at breakneck speed, almost knocking me out of the rocker pawing at me until Liz grabbed them and settled them down. We spent the next few days together, just the three of us, playing Candy Land and Chutes and Ladders, eating Cheerios in the living room, and becoming our own definition of a modern American family.

Amid the three-day Saunders family love fest, I juggled phone calls from Marty, Peter, and Ray.

Marty had to leave and get back to his job at Wal-Mart before they held it against him that he'd been gone so long on such short notice. From what I understood, Peter drove him to the train station. I was glad I didn't have to be in the car during that drive, but at least I had a chance to talk to Marty one last time before he went back home. He offered me money, time, more money, and still more money. Money he didn't really have to offer, but I appreciated the gesture all the same. He'd felt responsible for the pregnancy, and now he felt responsible for the miscarriage. In his view, I was meandering through my life, letting things happen to me because I was too nice to stop them. It was ridiculously overblown and over-simplified, but I loved him for believing it.

"Seriously, Em, if you want me to hang around or come back or something, I'll find a way to make it work."

"Marty, you know what I'm going to say."

He sighed. "I know, I know. But ... I want to help."

"Just help by staying my friend. Don't let us go so long before staying in touch from now on."

"Can I friend you on Facebook?"

I snorted. "Sure."

"Awesome."

"I've got about a thousand friends on Facebook, Marty."

Silence. "Really?"

"Don't get intimidated. Most of them are from my denomination. We're very close."

He chuckled on his end of the line. "Apparently."

"You can follow me on Twitter, though."

"Don't do me any favors."

"Never in a million years."

He sighed audibly. "I love you."

"I know. Me too."

"You love you too?" he teased.

"Actually, no, I don't love me. Not really. Not today."

"Maybe you'll love you tomorrow then."

"Maybe."

+ + + + +

As I WISTFULLY HUNG UP THE PHONE when Marty and I were done talking, I knew it was the right thing for us to be apart now. I had problems to solve and wrongs to right, and I had to do it on my own. I needed—and wanted—a kind of spiritual supervision that I'd never get from Marty.

Peter was more subdued about his offers of help. He offered once, most sincerely, and then backed off for a while to let the womenfolk handle things more efficiently and lovingly than he could. And handle things they did. Meg brought her famous meals—mostly casseroles of poultry, other meats, rice or pasta, and various creams and sauces, along with homemade breads and rolls—and galvanized an army of my favorite church ladies to take turns lavishing enough food on us to feed a small third-world country. She also left the house cleaner than she found it every time she visited. Mikey and Faith looked forward to her semi-daily visits, and we all felt mommied by everyone's care and concern. My only worry was that the kids would start to get used to this higher level of cooking and my own culinary prowess would forever be called into question.

Cassie made sure Faith and Mikey were properly cared for as well. She offered to do a few loads of laundry each week for a while, which I gratefully accepted. I made her leave the folding for me, though. It felt therapeutic to sit in the rocker in front of some truly bad television shows—which were legion during the day—folding clothes for the kids and me and putting them into neat little piles on the coffee table. Faith quickly learned how to take each pile and put it in its proper dresser drawer: Mikey's, hers, or mine. We made it a game, and she played it eagerly and well. She was happy I was on the road to recovery from what she viewed as my close brush with death. It never occurred to her that I was making her do *chores*. I secretly hoped her naiveté would last till she was in college.

Pastor Ray had called me not long after I got home—tentatively, tactfully, in that way only someone like Ray could get away with. Although I really didn't wish to discuss my sins while I was soaking maxi-pads at the rate of one an hour, his approach to the situation was wonderfully gracious. I could tell by the way he started out asking me things that he had an inkling of what really happened. My guess was that I came off sounding too guilty for someone who had supposedly been raped. When he suggested that I officially seek out biblical counseling for my ongoing struggles, I knew he suspected the truth. Amazingly, I was more relieved than worried. I wouldn't have been able to carry on the charade a whole lot longer, baby or no baby. And I certainly shouldn't have, either.

During the month that followed the miscarriage, Ray talked me through the circumstances that had led to the attack in the first place: the reunion, meeting Marty at the reunion, the fateful walk outside after the reunion. It wasn't quite time to start forgetting it all. But in a way, I'd already practiced telling the story to Liz after getting home from the hospital, so retelling it to Ray—with a few minor adjustments for decorum—wasn't as intimidating as it might have been. It started, though, with that initial phone call the day I got home.

"Can I come visit you there in the hospital?" he had asked, quietly.

"I'll probably be coming home either later today or first thing tomorrow morning. Might be better to nix the idea for now."

"Fair enough. I'll let you get your rest. I suspect you need it."

I breathed out a snarky laugh. "You have no idea."

"I might have more idea than you realize."

I balked. "Well ... you just might."

"And that's okay."

"And that's okay?" I echoed.

"Sure. You've been through a lot."

"Ray, it's not what you've been thinking ..."

"And how do you know what I've been thinking, young lady?"

I could hear the playful humor in his voice, one of the things the whole congregation loved about him. He had a sort of sixth sense about these things. I swear they must've taught this stuff at the seminary, probably had a whole course on it: Using Humor to Circumnavigate Panic in Your Church Members 101.

"Okay, so I don't know what you've been thinking. But let's face it: everybody's been think—"

"Don't over-analyze this, Emily. One step at a time."

"But you don't understand. Back in Easton, back when I was attacked ... I wasn't really—"

"I know."

"You know?"

"I saw you with your friend Marty. I have eyes. And ..."

"And?" I asked, hopefully.

"And it's all right."

"How can you say that? It's obviously a sin."

"I'm not saying that part's all right. But I could tell you've already dealt with it."

I snorted. "Not by a long shot."

"I meant, dealt with it between you and God."

I didn't know what to say, so I let the silence hang between us.

"I'm right, aren't I?" The gentleness in his voice was excruciatingly comforting. I closed my eyes and took a deep breath, the phone still cradled against my ear.

"Yeah. It all hit me pretty much right away. And hit me pretty hard. I felt ... awful."

"Of course you did. I would have expected you to beat yourself up over it—beyond what repentance might require. My guess is you always do. Am I right?"

He'd hit the bull's-eye again. I said nothing.

"Emily, I'd like to talk to you a little more—in person, and with Holly if you'd like—once you're home and have had a chance to recuperate and settle in. I'm not as concerned about what happened in Easton between you and Marty as I am about your tendency to flog yourself and second-guess your own life so much."

"Meaning what?" I asked, trying not to feel defensive.

"Meaning, you tend to think everyone's more spiritual than you are, better than you are. Truth is, we all struggle with different things before God. Your struggles aren't worse than mine. They're just different."

"I'm pretty sure mine are worse. That I'm worse."

"And I'm pretty sure you're not. We'll talk. Later. For now, remind yourself that you're forgiven and get some rest. That's an order."

I sighed. "Okay."

"And we can include Peter in our follow-up conversation, if you'd like."

"No, not Peter."

"Something wrong between you two? Doesn't he understand the ... situation?"

He'd hesitated just enough to make me feel uncomfortable again.

"Not yet, no. I haven't told him anything yet. I'm not sure ... well, I'm not so sure about ... us."

"I see." He was quiet for a moment. "Well, no worries about that for now, dear one. Rest. But do find a way to talk to him about ... things."

"Yeah, I will."

"God bless, Emily. You know the church is here for you. Always."

"I know. Sometimes I forget, but ... I know."

28

AS RAY RIGHTLY SUSPECTED, the hard part of the ongoing battle was going to be forgiving myself. The second hardest part was going to be telling Peter. Telling Peter something, *anything*. The first of these difficult communications—between myself and God—was done quietly, silently, and over a period of years. Repentance for me had always been a constant, vigilant struggle. The second was started by Peter, not me, and ended the same Saturday afternoon it started, on the way back from a psalm-sing in Eastvale.

✝ ✝ ✝ ✝ ✝

I LEANED BACK IN THE PASSENGER SEAT of Peter's Bronco and sighed again. There was silence from the back seat where the kids were safely belted in. I pulled down the visor mirror and tipped it to look into the back seat to confirm that Mikey and Faith were both asleep.

"How were they for you?" I asked Peter, who had shared nursery duty with several others at the psalm-sing.

"Fine. Mikey cried a little. I told him you would be back soon and that this was our special 'big guy' time, but I think he's too young to appreciate that."

"Probably."

I laughed and relaxed a little.

"I was thinking," Peter started. "You never said too much about your class reunion, your time with Marty. How did that go?"

I opened my eyes but kept my gaze out the side window. I wasn't prepared for this. Here I sat with nothing rehearsed, and I desperately wished I had tried to concoct a workable story that had enough elements of truth to get me by without being zapped by lightning from God. As things stood, the best I could do was continue to stare out the window and feign total fatigue and lack of attention. I didn't play my cards.

"Hmm?"

"Emily, c'mon. You've been back over two months, and you haven't said two words about the whole weekend."

I sat straight up and cleared my throat. "Peter, are we dating?"

"What?"

His eyes were back on the road and I could tell this was a potentially dangerous place to break the news, so I thought I'd divert his attention away from the reunion and Marty and deflect it back onto our own relationship first. I was going to need all the troops I could muster for this battle.

"I said, are we dating? You and me. What are we, exactly?"

"What do you mean, 'What are we?'"

He was frowning now, a rare look for him. I couldn't tell if he was upset, confused, or angry. The next few exchanges would tell.

"I mean, I know what the rest of the congregation thinks we are, but how close are they? We never talk about it—not as much as the rest of them do, I'm sure."

"Emily, I have no idea why a question about your class reunion would prompt this kind of answer. I'd answer you right away, but I feel like you're about to trap me into something, and frankly, it's not a very good feeling."

"Work with me here," I said animatedly, and pulled one leg up onto the seat, tucking it under the other leg and turning toward Peter slightly, gesturing with my hands. "I mean, we don't talk long-term at all. We've never made plans. We just sorta started hanging out and doing things together, and then we started taking the kids with us more, and suddenly I turn around and you're in the house at bedtime and tucking them in and they're asking you to read them bedtime stories once in a while. It feels like one thing, but in whole areas, nothing ever changes."

Peter kept frowning and was breathing through clenched teeth. "What are you implying? Are you saying I've been misleading you?"

"No," I began.

"Well then," he interrupted, now downright frustrated. "What's the point? And what does any of this have to do with your reunion? With Marty?"

It seemed the more I tried to focus in on the Peter and Emily Show, the more Peter seemed determined to tie it in with Marty and the reunion. Obviously I hadn't segued deftly enough, and he picked up on the mental disconnection I was trying to make in his mind.

"I'm just trying to define us a little. I think it's about time."

I felt as if I were drowning, and I had this sinking feeling that there wasn't going to be anything to grab onto on the way under this time.

"Why do you suddenly need to define us? Why now? This has something to do with Marty, doesn't it?"

I let the silence settle for a minute. He was going to let me drown myself and knew he didn't need to hold my head under. It was going to happen all on its own.

"What makes you say that? Sure, it was nice to see him again ..."

If this had sounded any more hollow, I would have heard an echo in the car.

"Nice to see him again? Emily, what's going on? You're being evasive."

I said nothing. I wasn't entirely sure what Peter was thinking, what he was fearing, but I began to hope desperately that whatever conclusion he was jumping to, that it was worse than the actual truth. Then I realized that Peter probably wasn't thinking anything nearly as bad as the truth, and the fear crept back into my mind.

"What do you mean, 'What's going on?'"

The stalling was beginning to get old, even to me.

"Emily, are we even having the same conversation? What happened between you and Marty? Did you guys have a big fight about religion again?"

It became painfully obvious that Peter had no idea which direction this conversation was going to go. He was still thinking in terms of religious squabbles, not unfaithful rolls in the hay behind his back. I wasn't even sure anymore why I was trying to get Peter to define our relationship when I could have done a better job. We were certainly an item, even if no one at church had ever winked or nudged or said a single thing. Physically there hadn't been anything beyond goodnight kisses, and even those were antiseptic and chaste. But no one would have categorized us any differently than a courtship, myself included. It wasn't until I left town and saw Marty again that I realized how shallow my feelings for Peter really were, religious similarities or not.

"No, there wasn't much talk about religion at all. In fact, I didn't even feel inclined to start any fights with him. We joked about it, but nothing ever happened."

I heard the double entendre as soon as I said it, but I knew that Peter wouldn't have picked up on it, stuck as he was on my obvious inability to be a faithful witness for Christ. He had no idea exactly how faithless I really was, did he?

"So is that what you've been afraid to tell me—that there's nothing to report? That you didn't even talk to him about God?" He sounded very frustrated and angry—for Peter, that is—and I still couldn't tell if he was angrier at the fact that I'd let Marty down, or that I'd been trying to cover it up for the last half hour or so.

"Well, no. Peter, can we talk about this later? We're gonna have to interrupt ourselves to get the kids out of the car in a few minutes when we get home, and by that point I just won't want them to wake up and hear what we're talking about because it's not going to be pleasant."

So now I'd set the timeline for the Big Blowout and couldn't back out. Peter just sighed, a heavy, manful sigh stuffed with that lack of power that women hand men when they put off important conversations. He said nothing but kept driving at an even rate of speed. The car had never crept above the speed limit the entire time we were talking and driving. Peter seemed able to segment his brain and keep himself out of danger while maintaining supreme frustration and anger. I wasn't sure I could multitask that well and was glad I wasn't the one driving. But, to be safe, I was still glad that the bigger bombshells wouldn't fall until we were inside and the kids were on a different floor of the house.

Peter was rounding the last corner before my house, and I realized that there was now little time to gather my remaining thoughts—incoherent and disparate as they now were—before we would be inside and talking about the Big Topic. He hadn't said a thing the rest of the trip, and the few times I gathered the compunction to look sidelong at him, he was still frowning and pursing his lips into a brooding little circle. Now that we were on my street, I ventured a last gaze at him while driving, and he was still in that same pose, holding that same gaze. I began to wonder if he had frozen that way. His mother probably warned him a million times about something like this happening. I stifled a nervous giggle, then realized that Peter heard it and was glaring at me from the driver's seat, even as he pulled into my driveway. He stepped heavy on the brake and the car pulled up short, lurching the two kids forward just a little, enough to jostle them awake from their nap.

"Where are we?" Faith asked, rubbing her eyes and sitting up straighter to see out the back window. "Home?"

I turned around. "Yep, honey, we're home already. Get out of that seatbelt and help wake up your brother, okay?"

I hurriedly undid my own shoulder belt and opened my door, glad for the distraction of managing the kids into the house, which would give me an opportunity to avoid Peter's face for just a while longer.

Opening Mikey's door, I caught him just as he slid back against the side of the car seat. The seatbelt pulled up and caught him just before I did, waking him.

"Ouch," he mumbled halfheartedly. "Mommy?" he said, and held his arms up to dump them across my shoulders. I pulled him close to me around his waist and he instinctively wrapped his little legs around my middle, monkey-like, sliding his head onto my shoulder and sighing, shifting just enough to get comfortable. He grunted a few times, rearranged himself on my shoulder, held onto my neck a little more tightly, but refused to wake up fully.

"You take him in," Peter said, "and I'll get Faith inside for you."

Hoisting Mikey up higher onto my shoulder, he still didn't rustle. I walked Mikey over to the couch for a moment, thinking I would deposit him there, then thought better of it, given the upcoming main event in this room within the next half hour, and instead walked upstairs and into their room, pushing open the door with my foot as I walked. Mikey fell silently on the bottom bunk, instinctively turned over onto his left side, facing away from me, and sighed one of his perpetually contented sighs and continued sleeping.

I straightened and looked at him a moment, wanting desperately for life to be that simple for me again, if only for the next day or so. Stretched out before me now was a task I brought on myself, and yet one I was in no way prepared to tackle. Funny how a person gets herself into these things.

Lingering there next to Mikey's bed, I wanted the rest of the house, if not the rest of the world, to go away. Outside this sanctuary of childhood was Peter, the guise of Marty, the troubles I caused, the hurt I was still causing, and the sin lying at the root of it all. Maybe I could just crawl into the bunk here next to Mikey, slide in behind him, curl up around him, feel him breathing that regular, still breathing of a soundly sleeping child, and not ever have to leave the room again.

A light tap at the bedroom door disturbed my musing. It was Peter carrying Faith, now also asleep, although more tentatively. He thought the same thing I did—that it was best for us to talk without the children lying sprawled around the living room furniture—and was walking past me to transfer her onto the top bunk as best he could. He rolled her off his shoulder and sideways onto the bunk, and she made a few grumbly noises and nearly awoke.

Peter turned to me and covered his mouth with one finger, motioning me to stay silent—as if I was going to strike up the band or something, I don't know. Leave the man alone with your kids for a few days while you go to a class reunion and suddenly he's an expert on how they stay asleep. I felt a defense mechanism coming on.

I nodded, somewhat annoyed, and turned and tiptoed out of the room. Faith would stay asleep if she hadn't awakened by this point. I wasn't about to stand there any longer now that the entire ambiance had changed.

As I made my way down the stairs, I heard the kids' door click closed quietly and then heard Peter's footfalls on the stairs behind me. I hit the first floor and kept walking, heading for the kitchen to get myself a beer out of the fridge. I stared inside the refrigerator as if I had no idea what I was looking at, trying to seem as intent and lost in thought as I possibly could, when all the while I was staring at eye-level at the beer I wanted. The same three pony bottles that had been sitting there for many months were still there. Peter didn't really look down on me for drinking, but he certainly would never have indulged in it himself.

I realized I had now embarked on a mental attitude fest and nipped it in the bud, fondling the Bud in my hand and finally closing the refrigerator door soundly. Peter was still standing behind me, having settled for a glass of water from the tap instead.

"Do you need that at this time of the afternoon?"

I didn't know what that meant. It was 4:30. It was obviously a more roundabout way of asking if I needed the alcoholic fortification to start the upcoming discussion. He was as edgy as I was by this point, and my own nervousness was playing off his.

"No, of course I don't *need* it, but I certainly have had an action-packed couple of months and I'd like to unwind a little. I'm not going anywhere after this, and I'm not driving, so yes, I am going to drink it and enjoy it. Are you okay with that?" I said, as snippy as necessary to be absolutely sure that this didn't turn into a lecture on alcohol and its applications for the layperson in the church.

"Never mind. I'll be in the living room if you want to talk," he said coldly and walked directly to the living room, past me and not brushing up against me, even inadvertently. Was this the out I needed? Could I just feign not having anything to talk about, or was he expecting for sure that I'd come in right behind him to start talking?

I was exploring options I didn't really have—I needed to do this—and I found my feet walking on their own, in step with Peter's, into the living room. Once there, I surveyed the available seats, and chose the rocker, as usual. He had already fallen onto the couch and had pulled one leg up and crossed it over the other ankle. He slung his right arm over the back of the couch, waiting for something to happen, for the show to begin. It was obvious I was supposed to say something.

"Well, how 'bout them Steelers?" I said, grinning, hoping to defuse a bit of the tension with a time-honored greeting in Pittsburgh.

I inhaled slowly before speaking, but Peter hadn't noticed since he was looking at his feet and fiddling with the shoelace of the foot crossed at the ankle.

"Emily, listen," he started, interrupting my inhalation, making me stop and hiccup slightly as I breathed back out. "I don't know what you're not telling me, how bad it is, whether it has anything to do with me or not. I don't want you to feel obligated to tell me just because I watched the kids ... or because we sit together at church ... or because ... well, because we have some sort of relationship."

"And what sort of relationship do we have?" I asked, more quizzically now, more honestly. Even he wasn't defining it at this point.

"I don't know why you need to know this now, but since you keep asking, I don't even know. I've told people we're seeing each other. They smile a lot. You know how they are. A few ask me when I'm going to marry you. I just smile back. I figure it's none of their business when I marry you."

"Or *if* you marry me," I corrected. The way he put that made me very uncomfortable suddenly, and he was sounding a bit too presumptuous for my liking.

"Well, yes," he said, rolling his eyes. "You know what I mean. What we are to each other isn't anyone else's business. There's no sinning, so there's nothing to tell, as far as I'm concerned. If that changes, they'll be the first hundred people to know."

"Okay, that sounds fair to me. What does it mean in terms of ... um ... in terms of what we tell each other?"

"Meaning?"

"Meaning, are we exclusive?"

He frowned again, and began pulling at his shoelace a little harder with his left hand, and scratching lightly at the tweed on the back of the couch with his right hand. "Emily, I wasn't expecting you to pull this out of your back pocket. I feel like I'm being set up here. Like there's a magic answer—the right answer—and then all the other possible answers. I wouldn't be surprised if a buzzer goes off once I tell you what I'm thinking."

I smiled. "Okay, I'm sorry I'm hitting you with this so hard, and from out of left field. It just sorta hit me in the car all at once, and I really just want to know all of a sudden. It's not like I'm pressing you too fast, though—we've been seeing each other for months now. And I get the same smiles and questions from people. 'When is that boy going to make an honest woman out of you?'"

Peter laughed out loud before he could check himself. "As if that would do it," he said.

I balked, but he continued laughing. He was joking. I kept forgetting all the stuff he still didn't know.

"Yeah, as if," I added, effecting a giddy spirit amid all the things still unsaid. "Anyway, have you thought about where we're going?"

"Yeah, a fair amount. And let me get this straight—you want to know all this before we talk about how your reunion went? Can you see how that would make a guy nervous?" He cracked a small smile, nothing elaborate or overblown, just simple and straightforward and unpretentious. He ran his left hand through his hair and began tapping his ankle rhythmically, nervously.

"Peter, what are you afraid of?"

"Okay, I know I haven't asked you to marry me. I know I haven't even whined about us not sleeping together, or even doing any heavy necking on the couch after the kids are asleep. I can see how that might mislead you into thinking I'm not interested in those things."

Now he was answering questions I hadn't asked. We were, it seems, suffering from the same malady: fear and a little panic. "Peter, this isn't about what you haven't said to me. I just really want to know. It just didn't seem as important to know before."

"Marty's a Christian now, isn't he?"

This struck me as if it were a sledgehammer blow to the head. "What?"

"Marty. He converted, didn't he? Either before you got there, or after he came here. Right?" He was obviously upset.

"What are you talking about?" I asked. "Besides, what could possibly make you upset about the prospect of Marty getting saved?"

He just stared at me. I hadn't answered his question, mostly because I wanted him to answer me first, but this sounded like dodging to Peter.

"Don't tell me. Let me guess. Marty is a Christian, and once you two saw each other again, you realized that now you could fall for each other. That's it, isn't it? He's a Christian, and he wins because you used to go roller skating together in high school or something."

Peter's shoelace was untied by this point, and he was loosening and tightening the shoe with one hand, poking and pulling and tugging at it, trying to get it just right, whatever that meant to him.

"As a matter of fact, Peter, no, Marty is no closer to Christ now than he was the last time I saw him—at least from what I could gather for the few days he was here. And if it makes you feel any better, we

didn't even talk much religion. I screwed up with Marty big-time."
Extremely poor choice of words, Emily.

Peter's countenance lightened considerably, and I felt guilty for allowing him a false sense of security, even if only for a moment. I'd taken away the short-term awkwardness by denying his worst fear, and was now going to offer him an alternative more gruesome to someone like him: sleeping with the enemy.

"I'm sorry, Em, I didn't realize. I just thought, and I mean, what with the question about us and all, and your not wanting to talk about it and all that ..."

He was not very good at fumbling over his words, more used to open vulnerability and no hiding behind speeches. I helped him out of his predicament.

"No problem. I can see how I gave you that impression. That I was going to run away with Marty or something. Trust me—that's not ever going to happen. Even if Marty does convert."

He sensed the dull thud of my voice, the defeat in it. "I'm sorry, Em. I was being pretty selfish. Sometimes I kick myself for not asking you to marry me before. I was sure I'd had my chance and taken it for granted and blown it."

"Well, I'm still me, and things can pretty much go on as they were, I guess." I listened to myself say this and wondered if I was going to jump in and tell Peter about sleeping with Marty. Suddenly, the bomb seemed not only defused but nonexistent. I didn't allow myself to hope that things would stay this way.

"Well, no, things can't continue the way they were. That's pretty obvious to me," he said.

He was fiddling with that shoelace again with both hands this time, looking intently at his task as if he were a neurosurgeon.

"Why not?" I felt a sudden buzz of adrenaline in my throat, the pulse pounding there. I knew Peter well enough to know that he was arming a bomb of his own.

"You certainly deserve to know what my intentions are. As for the rest of the church, they can figure it out on their own ... and they will."

He was smiling now, but still playing with his sneaker. Now he was lacing and unlacing the top eyelet. Abruptly he stopped, looked me squarely in the eye, and took in a deep breath.

"Emily, I think we *should* get married."

"Hmm?" I squeaked out, eyebrows raised up high, voice cracking, heart pounding. "We should what?"

"Get married. I think we should get married. Don't you?"

So, instead of proposing, he was asking me my opinion on the subject. How romantic.

"Um, Peter ... I mean, this is sorta ... well ..."

"Okay, wait, let me rephrase that: Emily, will you marry me?" he said hastily, slumping off the couch onto the floor, one knee down, the other up. I gaped at him, gasping somewhat and unable to take him as seriously as he was taking himself.

"Will I what?" I asked, even though I'd heard him just fine.

"Marry me ... will you marry me?" he asked again, with even less romance oozing from his pores than the first two times, and in fact with a slight edge of annoyance in it, if my emotional radar was up and working properly.

"Peter," I began, sighing heavily.

"You're going to say no, aren't you?" he interjected.

"Fine. You don't really need me here, do you? You can ask the questions and answer them too. How convenient."

"I'm sorry," he offered. Putting him on the defensive at a time like this was downright cruel. I wasn't liking the person I was fast becoming at his expense. I needed to put a quick and painless stop to this charade, or at least part of it.

"Peter, I can't marry you. Well, I mean, I can't do that to you."

"Emily, don't pull the self-esteem baloney on me. We've been over the blue-blood stuff and the used merchandise crap before. You know that stuff doesn't bother me."

"Peter, that's not what I'm talking about. You would regret marrying me. Trust me. This I know," I said emphatically and reached to the end table for the Budweiser.

Peter stood straight up. "Fine. Then what have we been doing here all these months? How can you sound so sure about this all of a sudden?"

I got up in response to his standing and then walked past him and back out to the kitchen with my beer.

"Peter, this isn't something I've been plotting. But I am sure about it. We just aren't cut from the same cloth. I don't see that changing."

He was, of course, right behind me. "Em, I don't want to argue you into this, but I think I deserve a better explanation than this."

I turned and looked at him a moment, then nodded quietly and a bit sadly. "If I tell you everything I'm thinking, I'll be surprised if you'll still talk to me. But it'd be better than us getting married."

Peter turned crisply on his heels and headed to the archway near the front door. He picked up his keys off the sideboard and stepped right up to the door, then turned. I was right behind him, knowing I was showing him out, and he startled me with his abruptness.

"You're not fooling, are you? We're not getting married, ever."

"I doubt it," I said coolly. Then I realized that he seemed more perturbed than curious or interested.

"Fine," he said curtly and opened the door, stepping outside and heading down the front steps without so much as looking back.

"Peter?" I called after him. He turned around and stopped, shielding his eyes from the overhead sun from the west. I wasn't sure if he could see me properly with the glare he must have had in his eyes.

"What?"

"Don't you want to know what happened ... at the reunion?"

He dropped his hand, looked at the ground, kicked up a small patch of dirt around a flagstone, and spat onto the cold grass. Raising his hand to reshield his eyes, he looked my way again, seeing me or not, I didn't know.

"Nope."

He turned and got into the Bronco quickly and efficiently, not making eye contact with me again. I watched him start the car and back out of the driveway, unable to call out to him to stop. I blinked back a few tears, not knowing if they were Peter tears, or Marty tears, or even Jonathan tears.

+ + + + +

LATER, I SAT AT THE KITCHEN TABLE with my second beer, cradling it carefully but not drinking it. The silence was deafening. I'd just gotten off the phone with Meg, who'd told me some surreal news about my favorite person, Everett Newman. I quietly thanked God that my memory of the attack had never returned. Maybe I'd get lucky and I wouldn't have to testify. Maybe he'd plead guilty and it would all end with a whimper and not a bang. What was wrong with that man? Had he really hated me that much? I shuddered.

No matter what, I'd have the support of a whole boatload of people to help me through whatever came next. I'd probably even have the support of Janie Newman, God bless her.

But right now, as I sat here processing the afternoon's exchange with Peter and the conversation with Meg, there weren't going to be enough beers in the world.

And suddenly I realized I was exhausted. Completely drained, unlike the beer I was still nursing. It was a good thing tomorrow was the Lord's Day. I needed more refreshment than this beer was ever going to give me.

The End

About the Author

IN THE EARLY 1980S, Linda pursued a writing degree from Carnegie Mellon University in Pittsburgh, Pa., but never quite finished. She has since worked behind the scenes in publishing as a proofreader, typesetter, and copy editor. She's worked with publishers, big and small, and with individual authors, big and small. She's also an 8th grade composition coach for WriteAtHome.com.

Linda is currently on the board of the St. Davids Christian Writers' Association and the board of education and publication of the Reformed Presbyterian Church of North America. She also serves as author liaison for the Beaver County BookFest in Pennsylvania.

Linda also enjoys comedy, computer gadgets, office supplies, reading, movies, adventure games, crocheting—and her office guinea pigs, who keep her company while she's working. She currently lives in western Pennsylvania with her husband, Wayne Parker. They share six children between them, all of them now grown and living their own adventurous stories.

One chapter of *Gray Area* won first place in Adult Fiction at the St. Davids Christian Writers' Conference. The entire novel placed as a semifinalist in the national contest Operation First Novel in 2005.

77580797R00133

Made in the USA
Columbia, SC
01 October 2017